I0586186

## LEGACY OF AN OUTLAW (THE PEACEKEEPER)

"Poston's [Jason] Peares walks into trouble at every turn. He's tough, quick with a gun, and understanding of the underdog."

—Steven Havill, author of *Privileged to Kill*

"A fast-moving story of guns and gunfighters, with a climactic cattle stampede of Texas-caliber proportions."

—Elmer Kelton, author of *Cloudy in the West*

"An exciting, page-turning traditional western sure to please. Fine work."

—Norman Zollinger, author of *Rage in Chupadera*

"Poston's stylishly written action yarn will generate a strong following among western fans."

—Wes Lukowsky, American Library Association

## COURAGE

"Jeffrey Poston understands the craft of constructing his novel and does a wonderful job balancing narrative elements with his dialogue. When his protagonist handles his firearms, you know the author has done his research in describing the action."

—Phillip Hardy, Lulu.com review

## A MAN CALLED TROUBLE

"In his first novel, Jeffrey A. Poston has numbered himself among the best writers of westerns working today."

—Biblio.com review Praise for Jeffrey Poston

## WARRIORS

"It doesn't get any more real than this."

—D. Brock, Silver City, NM

# BOOKS BY JEFFREY POSTON

## ACTION/ADVENTURE THRILLERS

*American Terrorist: Where is the Girl?*
*Contagion: American Terrorist 2*
*Escalate! American Terrorist 3*
*American Terrorist Trilogy*

*Joshua Experiment (Call Sign: Raven Book 1)*
*The End of Everything (Call Sign: Raven Book 2)*
*The Queen (Call Sign: Raven Book 3)*

## JASON PEARES HISTORICAL WESTERNS

*Courage (Book 1)*
*Legacy of an Outlaw (Book 2)*
*Warriors (Book 3)*
*Manhunter (Book 4)*

# MANHUNTER

## A Jason Peares Western

# JEFFREY POSTON

LOMAS & TURNER PRESS

*Manhunter (A Jason Peares Historical Western Book 4)*
Copyright © 2014 by Jeffrey Poston, Lomas & Turner Press

All characters and events in this book, other than those clearly in the public domain, are fictitious and any resemblance to real persons, living or dead, is purely coincidental.

All rights reserved. No part of this publication may be reproduced, distributed, or transmitted in any form or by any means, including photocopying, recording, or other electronic or mechanical methods, without the prior written permission of the publisher, except in the case of brief quotations embodied in critical reviews and certain other noncommercial uses permitted by copyright law. For permission requests, write to the publisher, addressed "Attention: Permissions Coordinator," at the address below.
Lomas & Turner Press
www.JeffreyPostonBooks.com

Ordering Information:

Quantity sales. Special discounts are available on quantity purchases by corporations, associations, and others. Orders by U.S. trade bookstores and wholesalers. For details, contact the publisher at the address above.

Editing by The Pro Book Editor
Cover design by Deanna Dionne
Interior design by IAPS.rocks

eBook ISBN: 978-0-9916194-4-3
paperback ISBN: 978-0-9863328-5-2

    1. Main category—Fiction/Westerns
    2. Other category—Fiction/Action and Adventure

First Edition

# CHAPTER I

**B**LOOD PAINTED THE DIRT STREET of Rosebud, Colorado.

"I'd wager a year's crop you're glad I wear guns now, Sheriff," Jay said. He looked first at the dead body near his feet, then at the dead man on the boardwalk.

Sheriff Travers grunted. "I'm grateful, yes, but I still don't like it. And it don't change nothing."

The lawman began pulling shells from his pocket to reload his Winchester rifle. He looked at the dead men, then eyed the onlookers. Pedestrians and buckboard traffic were just beginning to return to normal.

"No casualties among the innocent," he said. "This time." Sheriff Travers looked Jay intensely in the eye, but Jay looked away respectfully. He didn't want to challenge his future father-in-law. Many angry words had passed between them over the months. Jay loved the sheriff's daughter, Joanne, and she loved him. He wanted her father's acceptance of that fact.

Travers looked him up and down, as if studying his worth before finally resting his gaze on the two guns tucked in Jay's belt. Jay was tall and thin, yet tightly muscular. His short black hair, mostly hidden under his hat, was slightly curly. Black folk called his complexion "high yella," while White folk just called him Negro. Sometimes folks called him "half-breed"—a name he'd learned to hate over the years—but that was rare. Especially when he wore his double-gun rig.

"I don't reckon I have much to complain about today," the

sheriff said. "At least not about your ability to handle a gun. But what you're askin' of me is…well…it's too hard for any father to take. I don't want to see my daughter takin' up with…your kind."

"I'm not an outlaw anymore," Jay said gently. "Haven't been for almost seven years now."

Travers shook his head. "I'm talkin' about those guns. It don't seem right lettin' my little girl marry a gunfighter. It just isn't the way things ought to be. When you live by the gun, you most likely will die by the gun. I don't want to see her have to suffer through that."

Jay considered the irony of the advice given by a sheriff, a married man who also lived by the gun. The sheriff looked to his right at a couple of preteen boys standing on the boardwalk, imitating the gun battle. One of the boys emptied his make-believe finger gun into the chest of the other, then coolly blew imaginary smoke from his fingertip. The other croaked loudly, mortally wounded, then fell to one knee.

"You two!" The sheriff gestured angrily to the boys. "Quit playin' around and start dragging these bodies over to the undertaker."

The boys jumped to their task as Joanne walked into the middle of the street to join Jay and her father. She hugged Jay and started to say something but was interrupted by the warning shout from the east end of the street. More riders were coming.

Jay turned and started to pull a gun as the group came around a corner, far up the street. He saw the sunlight reflect off metal on the vests of the two front riders and he relaxed. Nine lawmen in all, the posse rode carefully and deliberately up the street. All wore black hats and long gray coats and they spread out in the main street.

Jay turned back to Joanne and her father. His fiancée was clearly uncomfortable, sensing the tension between Jay and her father. Travers pumped shells into his rifle.

"Sheriff," Jay said. "I love Joanne, and I want to marry her. And I'd like your blessing."

The unspoken message was clear. Jay planned to marry

Joanne whether he had her father's approval or not. The lawman stopped what he was doing and stared at Jay for long moments. He took a deep breath and stood taller as if preparing to meet Jay's defiance with equal stubbornness. Then he simply cradled his rifle under his right arm and hooked his left thumb inside his suspender strap where it buttoned onto his trousers.

He started to speak but was distracted—his gaze drawn just over Jay's shoulder to the group of lawmen approaching half a block away. Jay had just started to turn, to see what was causing the intensifying look of concern growing in the sheriff's eyes, when he barely heard the familiar voice. It was deep and husky, and it triggered a whisper of a memory from years past.

"It's him!"

Jay slowly narrowed his eyes and turned his whole body toward the riders, the familiar panic of fear gripping his insides even before his eyes met those of the lead rider.

"You!" Jay said more as a forced, panicked whisper than a shout.

Jay drew his guns without thinking and started shooting. Explosions of guns and rifles shattered the stillness of the afternoon as the lawmen pulled their weapons and returned fire. Shouts and cries of pain and fear echoed in Jay's ears. He heard the zip of bullets pass by close to him, then felt pain rip into his body two, three times. He stumbled but kept shooting. Then the ground slammed into him.

Everything became quiet and dark and cold. Jay felt a strange sensation of surprise in the last fraction of a second as he relinquished his hold on consciousness. The end hadn't come as he had expected it to. He'd always expected to have time to prepare for that last glorious gunfight. Maybe he'd have time to consider his possibility of success or failure. Maybe he'd have time to reflect on how he might be remembered.

In reality, the end came suddenly and without warning. He'd had no time to think of anything, no time even to feel the force of bullets tearing into his body, hammering him to the ground.

# CHAPTER 2

## FIVE DAYS PREVIOUS

CHARLES STRANGE PEERED THROUGH HIS spyglass at the distant town of Willow Bend. It sprawled over ten criss-crossing roads, three of which linked the west side of town with the east side, over the winding creek that split the town almost evenly into two halves. It was a critical flaw in town planning, Strange thought. The sheriff's office was on the west side of town, and the bank was on the east.

Only once each year would Strange's plan have a prayer of a chance of success, and he knew that opportunity was today. The huge holding pens north of town were filled to the bursting point from the cattle drive, which had arrived that very morning from down Texas way. The bid on over three thousand head, at a bit over two dollars apiece, had just taken place. Payment had changed hands. Cattle hands had been paid and were rushing off to give away a sizable chunk of their earnings to the saloons and other establishments for booze and whores.

Strange rose from his squat atop the boulder. He took a deep breath of the cool, crisp air and looked once more at the town four miles away. From his vantage point in the hills just south of town, he could see the entire lay of the land north of him, from the canyon where he stood to the mountains bordering the wide valley. Those mountains merged together south of the wide valley in a nearly impassable wall of rock and canyons. It was into that maze of canyons and crevasses Strange's band of criminals would disappear after their caper. He knew by the time anyone found their escape path, he and his men would already have a week's head start. No one would ever find them.

Charles Strange turned to his twelve waiting men. He stood before the silent group and looked at each man for a few seconds. His brand of leadership spawned absolute loyalty and discipline. Extreme fear and extreme rewards were his tools. He never hesitated to kill one of his own to make an example for the rest, and he never failed to divide up the booty evenly between all his men. Strange never had to worry about turning his back on his men because he also made sure they all knew of a very important story.

Three years ago, one of his men mutinied, but failed to kill him. In retaliation, Strange killed not only the mutineer but also three others who'd failed to warn or defend him. Now, none of his men would let another attempt such a thing. It would be bad for their own well-being. So, Strange figured he was safe unless they all turned against him at the same time.

*What were the chances of that happening? Besides, what would the Strange Scalpers be without Charles Strange?*

He had taken in three new men recently. They were afraid of him and had heard all the rumors about him, but they hadn't been seasoned yet. One wiry, old man, about forty, always had a disbelieving look in his eyes. Silvan Thompson seemed to have taken the mantle upon himself to question orders. The man was scrappy in a fight, but absolute discipline was always just out of reach. Strange had always known he would have to make an example of the man one day.

"All right, everyone," Strange said. "The cattle arrived this morning up the southeast trail and are penned up north of town. The money arrived just now from across the river. They've inspected the animals, put out the lame ones, and worked up the payment. The foreman put the money in the bank. So after a good night's rest, he'll probably be ready to ride south.

"So all that money's just sitting in the bank, waiting for us. Let's review the plan again, just to make sure everyone knows what they're supposed to do. First?"

Barkley picked up a satchel and spoke up. "Me, Caruthers, and Longford are gonna go into town first and wire some dynamite to the three bridges crossing the river. When the first gunshots sound off, we'll blow the bridges. Snow melt's done swole up the creek somethin' fierce, and it's flowing way too fast for anyone to get across without using one of the bridges."

Strange nodded. "Good. Second?"

"That's me, boss." An older man, about fifty and carrying a bit too much weight around his midsection, pulled a pair of wire cutters from his back pocket. "I'll cut the telegraph wire so no one can wire for help."

"And third?"

"The sheriff's office is on the west side of the river," Roland drawled in a deep baritone voice. "So that's where the sheriff and his deputies will be trapped after the bridges are blown. The money's locked up in the bank on the east side of the river. The marshal's the only lawman with an office on our side of the river, so I'll take four men to make sure he doesn't interfere with our plans."

"Fourth?"

Another voice chimed up from the group. "Me and Hank'll be on the rooftops. I'll be on the bank, and Hank'll be on the church steeple up the road."

"And fifth, I guess that leaves you and me, Chris."

Strange nodded at Chris Kendrick, his longtime partner and second-in-command.

Chris said, "Yeah. We get to have the most fun of all."

Chris had one front bucktooth and the other front tooth was missing, so he spoke with a lisp. Many men had laughed once too often at the youthful looking, freckle-faced redhead before learning too late his baby face hid the temper of a ruthless and cold-blooded killer.

"We'll grab ourselves a hostage to discourage the guard from being a hero when we mosey our way into the bank. Then we'll shoot the guard and two of the hostages, women or children if there's any in there, so no one will doubt our commitment." He chuckled. "Then we'll grab all the money, take our hostage to the end of town, and wait for everyone to meet up."

Charles Strange finished the thought. "Then we disappear." He paused, deciding to spell out the details one last time, just for thoroughness.

"Okay, the sheriff has twelve deputies. Nine of them were on the east side with the money until they stuck it in the bank. Like Roland says, they all went back over the river for lunch, except for the one who is on guard at the bank. That leaves the marshal. He runs a one-man office next door to the courthouse." He directed his gaze at Roland. "And you'll see to it he doesn't leave the office." Roland nodded.

Strange looked around and took a few steps to his left. "Any questions?"

No one spoke, and Strange innocently glanced at Silvan Thompson, then spoke gently. "Silvan, you look like you have a question to ask." The older man glanced around sheepishly, but hesitated.

Strange reached out and patted him on the shoulder. "Go ahead, I won't bite your head off, you know. Ask your question."

Silvan nodded. "Well, boss, I was just wondering how you know—"

Several of the men who had been looking around or checking their weapons glanced up as Silvan stopped in mid-sentence. They noticed Strange was wiping his knife against his pant leg before carefully parking his blade back in its sheath on his hip. At first, Silvan just stood there, eyes wide open in shock and surprise. Then a thin, red line across his neck began to drip blood.

He tried to speak, but only coughed out a gurgling sound. Realizing Strange had sliced him clean to the bone, he reached for his neck as his legs wobbled under him. He fell to his knees.

Strange pulled a gun from his holster and cocked the

hammer back, pointing it at Silvan's head. "Anybody else have any questions?"

"I have a question."

A chorus of gasps followed, and everyone moved away from Hank Winters.

"You do?" Strange said. He had a look of complete disbelief as he turned to face Hank behind him. His gun was pointed perilously in Hank's direction.

"A favor, actually." Hank stepped forward. "Instead of shooting him, maybe we could just watch him for a while. You know, let him suffer."

"You don't like him much, do you?" Strange glanced over at Chris and smiled. Chris nodded and eased his hand to the gun tucked in his belt.

Hank knelt in front of Silvan as the man continued to claw silently at the grass, his blood gushing out of his split neck and soaking into the ground.

"He reminds me of my pa. The last few days since he came on, he was always barking out orders like he was running things."

Strange chuckled. "Men could say their pa done worse things." He wondered if Hank and Silvan were close. Charles Strange stepped in beside Hank and slid his knife free.

"Yeah, well my pa came home drunk more times than not and beat the crap out of me until I was twelve."

"What happened when you were twelve? You got up the nerve to run away?"

"Something like that. On my birthday he beat me real bad, then passed out drunk on the floor. I sat there in front of him all night and through the morning and into the afternoon, watching him, waiting for him to wake up. And when he did, I cut his throat." Hank paused and chuckled. "Just like this." He pointed at Thompson's twitching body. "Then I watched him die."

Strange leaned down and handed Hank his knife. "You have the duty, then."

"Duty? Hardly," Hank said, reaching for the knife. "It's a pleasure. They don't call us the Strange Scalpers for nothing."

Hank swiped the sharp blade twice, once on each side of Silvan's head, both times grating the blade against the man's skull. Then he forced the man face first into the mud and stood, placing his boot against the back of his head. He grabbed a handful of hair and stood upright, pulling the scalp off the now dead man with a wet, ripping sound. He held it aloft and received the cheer he expected from the rest of the men.

The deed complete, Strange nodded and retrieved his knife. He turned to Roland. "Looks like you'll have to deal with the marshal with only three men."

Derrick Gallagher sat with his boots propped up on the desk. He was reclined nearly prone in his office chair, with only the two back legs of the chair on the floor. He drifted slowly out of his nap as the scent of cinnamon invaded his nostrils. It was a strong scent, and he sneezed violently, a full-body convulsion with arms and legs flailing wildly, and almost fell out of his chair.

Elizabeth Gallagher screeched as the plate of cinnamon-seasoned apple pie she had held under his nose flopped upside down onto his chest.

"Now look what you've done," she said as she hurriedly tried to wipe the dessert from his vest and back onto the plate. He opened his eyes and lay still.

"Yes, I've done it now." He looked down at his vest. "Ruined a perfectly good piece of pie. What a waste."

"Oh, no you don't. I spent a lot of time and trouble baking this for you and bringing it to you. You're going to eat it if I have to shove it down your throat."

"I love it when you talk bossy like that."

Gallagher grabbed her and pulled her close in a hug, then reached down and grabbed a handful of her ample buttocks. She slapped his hand and backed away, feigning embarrassment.

"You be decent, Marshal, or I'll have you arrested."

"Why? There's never anyone around here to see. Just me."

He waved a hand around his tiny office. "There's nothing ever to do around here anyway."

"That's the way your job should be after forty years," Elizabeth said, pushing away from him. "And don't get pie all over me."

He watched her sashay over to the doorway. Now that he was seriously considering retiring, his wife had become even more attractive to him. He knew it was likely just the anticipation of a new lifestyle, of being around her much more, but he'd take the seduction any way it presented itself.

"Lizzy," he called after her. She turned and smiled sweetly. "I love you."

"Eat your pie," she replied as she turned to leave, but he called to her again while making his way from behind his desk. He retrieved a wad of money and went to the door to give it to her.

"Wanna stop by the bank and deposit my pay?"

"Sure." She kissed him lightly on the lips, the communication of a long, happy marriage in the eye contact. "Happy birthday. And don't forget to change your vest."

Marshal Gallagher went to the door and watched her walk up the boardwalk for a moment, then turned his attention to the rescued portion of his apple pie. He took an overly large bite and savored it as he tugged his way out of his stained vest. He retrieved another just like it from the tiny closet and buttoned it up, then pinned his circular badge to the front. He took another bite of pie, then examined himself in the full-length mirror beside the closet. He was meticulous about his appearance. Everything had to be perfect. In fact, he couldn't ever remember being anything other than perfect. It was going to take some practice giving up *perfect* in exchange for a leisurely retirement. There was no way Elizabeth would let him transfer his military-like orderliness from his office to the house.

He straightened his shoulder-length gray hair, noticing again how rapidly it seemed to be thinning out and receding, then finger-combed his drooping gray mustache and beard. He straightened his white shirt under the black vest, then repositioned his silver belt buckle in the exact center of his black trousers. His deep gray boots were clean and relatively free of dust.

Out of a decade's worth of habit, he unhooked the leather safety strap from the hammer of his gun as he prepared to leave his office and make his rounds. He tested the weapon for the ease of the draw. He was right-handed, so the single-gun holster hung low on his right hip. Another leather strap held the bottom of the holster securely to his thigh.

He grabbed his black hat from the rack and placed it perfectly horizontal atop his head. Then as he examined his appearance, he cocked the hat slightly forward and to the right as he always did, then headed for the door.

As an afterthought, Gallagher stuffed the last bit of pie in his mouth and checked the mirror again. He smoothed his still-black eyebrows in front of the mirror and removed a speck of pie from the corner of his mouth. As he stepped out onto the board-walk and closed the office door behind him, he finished chewing and swallowing, then took a deep breath of the cool mountain air. He scanned up and down the street, more out of habit than for any practical reason. Nowadays, people were fairly civilized around these parts. Several months had passed since even the last drunken brawl.

Mrs. Hanley, from the general store down the street, walked by and smiled at him. He tipped his hat respectfully. "Ma'am," he said, his attention already on another familiar figure walking his way.

The Black man was huge, easily standing a head higher than Gallagher, and was about as bowlegged as a man could be and not be crippled. There was easy confidence in his stride, but the smile that normally painted his dark features was absent.

"Good afternoon, Marshal," the man said.

Gallagher nodded. "Mr. Madison."

Bo Madison, his friend for as long as he could remember, was one of the few men who ever called Gallagher by his first name. The only time the two men were ever formal was when they were on the trail of an outlaw or when danger was near. Gallagher couldn't remember when they had developed that manner of code to warn the other of trouble, but it didn't matter. Each man trusted the other implicitly with his life, and each had saved the other's life more times than they could recount. As a result, their friendship was more akin to a brotherly love.

Gallagher passed Madison by without another word. He had seen the four riders across the street from his office watching him as he started his walk. Even as he stepped off the end of the covered boardwalk, he glanced sideways and saw them still watching him.

The last building on the block was the California-style courthouse. Its entrance was set back from the corner by a small courtyard with stone benches. The front of the courthouse was framed by pillars and seemed to be an overly large building for such a small town. However, the courthouse had been built with federal funds to handle local, state, and regional federal cases, as well as for other political business. Two prominent attorneys nodded at Gallagher as he paused at the corner and pretended he was trying to decide which way to walk.

Gallagher turned right and crossed the street, then headed back the way he had started. Now he faced the riders who had begun to follow him, two on horseback and two afoot. They seemed to sense they had been outmaneuvered as Gallagher centered his attention on them. Madison burst out of the marshal's office holding a sawed-off shotgun with a pistol grip in his massive right hand, and a rifle in his left. His voice boomed at the four men.

"Keep your hands clear of your weapons!"

They seemed to know they were trapped, but Gallagher saw in their eyes that the price for failure was too high for whatever their task was. They drew their guns. At fifty-eight years old, Gallagher's draw was nowhere near as fast as it was in his prime, but the lead man, Roland, was distracted by the sudden explosion of Madison's double-barreled shotgun. By the time Roland reacted, Gallagher had fired two bullets into his chest, knocking him from his horse. The big man still had fight in him and struggled to clear leather. Gallagher shot him four more times before the man finally collapsed. Then he watched Madison work his magic.

The man fired his rifle, then spun the weapon in his left hand like a gunfighter twirls a gun, working the lever in the same one-handed motion, and shot again. Four more times in the space of four seconds, Madison spun the rifle, shooting with one hand, until the other three men lay dead in the street. Then he pointed the rifle barrel to the sky with the empty shotgun pointed at the ground and walked over to the marshal.

"Happy birthday, Derrick. What is it this year, a hundred and two?"

"We're going to have to work on your counting skills." He fingered his gray beard. "And your eyesight. I look pretty good for thirty-five, don't you think?"

"Downright purty, if not delusional." Madison gestured to the dead men. "Friends of yours?"

"Not that I'm aware of. I wonder what all this was about."

"There's a lot of cattle around. A lot of money in the bank."

"But if these men were following me, then...." Gallagher began, his hands working automatically to reload his pistol from shells in his belt.

"Then they know you. That means there's some serious planning going on here. We should get over to the bank, just in case."

Gallagher nodded, remembering the bank was his wife's destination. He was just about to mention it to Bo Madison when three massive explosions erupted down by the creek. They ran to the corner just in time to see wood and debris from the bridges being swept away with the rushing current of the swollen creek. He heard the screams of folks wounded in the explosion of the nearest bridge and saw flailing arms in the fast-moving water. He and Bo had just started to run toward the blasts when gunfire erupted from the bank two streets over.

Charles Strange grabbed the redhead by the hair and nearly dragged her into the bank. The young sheriff on guard drew his weapon but hesitated for fear of hitting the woman. Strange did not hesitate. His gun barked twice. As the deputy fell, Strange looked around the foyer of the bank. Nearly a dozen people cowered along the walls, screaming or whimpering in fear. A mother sheltered her young daughter with her own body, and Strange smiled.

"Chris," he said quietly, nodding at the mother.

Chris nodded in return and emptied his gun into the two. Then he turned to the tellers. "Does anyone have any doubts about what we're capable of?"

The two men behind the metal bars over the counter shook their heads and trembled.

"Good. Then both of you get into the vault and fill some bags full of money. And be quick about it, or I'm going to have to kill some more of your customers."

Three minutes later, Chris had his hands wrapped around two large burlap sacks stuffed full of currency and coin.

"Trophies, Charles?"

"Damn straight," he said, then looked around at the cowering customers before adding the popular motto everyone in his group seemed happy to repeat. "They don't call us the Strange Scalpers for nothing."

Chris attended to the three dead bodies, then tied their dripping scalps to his belt and followed Charles Strange out to their waiting horses. Strange stopped just outside the door as gunfire erupted from Strange's rooftop lookouts. He could see Marshal Gallagher and a big Black man pinned down by merciless cross fire, shielded only by a buckboard. Neither man could even get off a shot, but still Charles Strange was not happy with the appearance of the two men. The marshal should have been dead, and the Black man was unknown to him. He'd accounted for all the deputies except for that man.

Strange smiled calmly and dragged the woman into the middle of the street. Despite this unexpected wrinkle, the plan had not been affected. He waved his free hand and all gunfire ceased. Another signal sent his men scrambling from their perches and to their horses. Chris mounted up and muscled the heavy burlap sacks over his horse's rump. As he tied the sacks down, Strange lifted the struggling woman across his partner's saddle.

Strange turned to face Gallagher as he and Madison stepped from behind the buckboard with weapons drawn. Gallagher took a step toward Chris's mount but stopped when he caught sight of the gun pointed at her back as she lay across his saddle.

"No more gunfire, gentlemen," Strange said calmly.

"So help me, if you—"

"Save your threats, Marshal," Strange said, trivially waving aside Gallagher's comments. "I think you understand the situation quite clearly."

Strange shrugged his shoulders and watched as his other men rode slowly toward the east end of the street. Chris followed them after a moment.

"It's as simple as this, Marshal. We'll not kill anyone else, if no one shoots at us. And if you kill me, your woman dies."

He watched the thoughts pass quickly over Gallagher's face. Confusion, anger, fear for his wife.

"Oh, yes. I know she's your wife. And I know all about your reputation. Truthfully, I didn't really believe my men would stop you from getting over here. It was just dumb luck she came to the bank. Saved me the time sending a man to visit your cabin to get her." He paused. "Now put your gun away."

He looked up the street to see his men turning to the south. Chris stopped at the end of the street and waited. Strange looked back at Gallagher, then glanced down at the gun still pointed at his chest.

"I said, put your gun away, Marshal." Strange nodded at Madison. "You too."

Gallagher holstered his weapon, and Bo Madison tossed his rifle into the street. Gallagher stepped close to Strange, their noses separated only by the brims of their hats. Strange was taller—almost as tall as Madison—and Gallagher looked up into his brown eyes.

Strange just grinned a smug look of confidence, but Gallagher unnerved him. He resisted the urge to step back and kept the fake look of confidence in his eyes. He knew all about the lawman, but he had outsmarted and outmaneuvered the famous Marshal Gallagher. He had total control of the lawman, but still he stood right here in Strange's face. And he scared him.

Suddenly, Strange felt cold inside. He didn't like to be scared. It was the ultimate insult. He would respond as he always did when insulted.

"You hurt her, and there's nowhere you can run I won't find you."

"You know who I am, Marshal?"

Gallagher spoke slowly. "I don't believe I've had the pleasure."

Strange smiled, despite his feelings of discomfort. "You will." He turned and mounted his horse, then rode to join Chris without another look back.

Gallagher watched the man all the way, knowing he was powerless to do anything for fear of endangering his wife. He held his breath and waited. Hard, wordless communication had passed through their final eye contact. He could see the man believed Gallagher would make good on his word. He knew that belief was the only thing that would keep his wife alive.

He saw Strange pause at the corner as people finally began to trickle out of the bank. He heard Madison ask if anyone knew who the robbers were.

Someone muttered, "One of 'em said they were the Strange Scalpers."

Gallagher froze, felt an invisible fist slam into his gut. He couldn't breathe, and his heart pounded in his chest as if ready to explode. He tried to take a step forward, but he couldn't move.

A gunshot split the distance. A knife blade flashed in the sun. A yell of victory echoed up the road.

Gallagher's legs collapsed under him as the pain in his chest became too great to bear. The sound of a great river of rushing water filled his ears. Light scorched his eyes, and he clutched his chest, unable to breathe. The sun exploded into a swirl of bright colors, then everything burst into a brilliant white flash accompanied by an unbearable screeching sound inside his skull. Pain such as he had never felt blinded him. Then he fell into darkness.

# CHAPTER 3

## THREE DAYS PREVIOUS

DERRICK GALLAGHER OPENED HIS EYES and took a deep breath. He instantly recognized the medicine-air smell of old Doc Mather's house. He looked around briefly, then sat up and maneuvered himself until his butt was on the side of the bed and his stocking feet rested on the floor. The squeak of the bed alerted the doctor at his desk near the window of the large room.

Doc Mather grunted his way out of the chair and hobbled over to the bedside.

"Look at me," the doctor commanded. Gallagher obeyed as the doctor bent over close to his face and looked deep into his eyes. "Who am I?"

"You're an ugly, old man with horse breath whose eye is still keen and hand still steady, with at least twenty good years ahead."

Gallagher spoke the words with no intent of humor. The doctor grunted, apparently satisfied Gallagher still had his wit and senses about him.

"For a while there, I thought your heart gave out on you."

The marshal looked at the floor between his feet and closed his eyes for a moment, but he couldn't bear what he saw in that darkness.

"It did."

"How do you feel?"

"I feel like killing some men."

Gallagher wrestled his way into his boots, then stood up slowly. He grabbed his hat and gun belt from the chair beside the bed. He paused, clutching his chest with his hand. He felt like somebody carved his heart of his chest and splayed it open on a chopping block.

The doctor followed Gallagher to the front door. "I'm real sorry about Elizabeth, Marshal. She was a good woman."

Gallagher said nothing as he stepped out into the evening sunlight and closed the door behind him. He scanned the crowd gathered in the doctor's front yard. Eight familiar faces, none under fifty years old, stared back at him solemnly. These men were his second family. He'd known most of them all of their adult lives. They'd all helped birth, raise, and marry off their kids. He'd helped bury some of their kids too. They'd helped him bury his only son—a sheriff murdered by a half-breed outlaw ten years back.

Eight of his nine original deputies from years past gazed back at him. They were known as Gallagher's posse, feared and respected back in their heyday. The only man not present was Chubs Malone—killed during their two-year hunt of, and by, the same outlaw who'd killed his son. Gallagher mentally tore Jason Peares from his mind.

"What is this?" Gallagher demanded of the men. All were armed to the teeth and behind them their mounts were packed and ready.

"We're ready to ride when you are, Marshal." Bo Madison spoke, but all the men nodded in unison.

All the men were dressed in the same trail garb. Black pants and white shirts, dark gray long coats, wide-brimmed black hats, black or gray boots. And all wore deputy badges on the lapels of their coats. Bo Madison stood at the front of the group, two long-barreled weapons ever-present in his hands. Matthew McDonnell stood behind him, sided by the redhead Slim Jim,

Moses Jackson, and Steve Pickens. To the left of the porch steps waited the brothers Billy and Robert Hutchinson and the nearly toothless Crazy Willie Smith.

They were all old and wrinkled, and all but Bo and Slim Jim carrying the extra weight of the years around their bellies. *A casual observer might call them old-timers,* Gallagher mused, *and maybe that observer would be right.* Gallagher would follow all of them to hell and back. He'd done so many times over the years, and he knew they would follow him as well. It was part of their motto: "Anywhere, anytime."

*Anytime but now,* thought Gallagher.

"Sorry, boys. This is personal." Gallagher reached to his vest and started to unpin his badge, but Madison's words stopped him cold.

"This isn't about you, Marshal, and it's not about Elizabeth." He paused for a moment. "They killed seventeen in total, Derrick. When they blew up the bridges, six children fell in and drowned in the rushing, freezing water. Five more cattle drivers were lost in the river. They shot three innocent people outside the bank and a woman and her seven-year-old daughter inside, probably just to prove a point." He paused. "And Lizzy."

"He...," Gallagher's voice broke, "scalped her." He took a deep breath. "Because of me."

No one spoke.

"It's my fault she's dead. I scared him. I could see it in his eyes. He needed to be in control, and I challenged him. He knew I would hunt him down. And he killed her because he knew *I knew* he was scared." His voice crackled and he paused. "It's my fault."

"You know as well as I do he would have killed her anyway. That's his nature. It's not personal, Derrick," Madison said quietly. "The victims will be avenged, but justice must be served."

Gallagher glared at his best friend for a long time. Finally, he took a deep breath and collected himself. He nodded.

"Agreed. We'll handle this like the professionals we are." He saw several of his men stand just a bit straighter. "Let's meet back at my office. We'll need maps."

Moses Jackson held out a roll of maps to Gallagher.

Gallagher smiled faintly. "Always a step ahead, eh, Moses?"

Moses Jackson shrugged. "Well, I'll be needing my horse and pack."

Moses pointed off to the right where Gallagher's black stallion waited with the other horses.

"My trail clothes?"

Moses pointed to a bundle on the porch beside the door.

"Well, then, gather around, and let's get a plan brewing."

The men all quickly agreed on the obvious. Charles Strange had studied the town well in advance. The robbery was planned well and executed without flaw. By blowing the bridges, Strange had given himself several days head start on the posse. South of town, there were at least ten different hard-rock trails out of the mountains. Without the wildest stroke of luck, it would be impossible to find the trail they took. Even if Gallagher's men did get lucky and find the right trail, it would be nearly impossible to track them over the rocky terrain.

Bo nodded and summarized. "It looks like this one's going to be a long, hard trail to follow. We'll have to backtrack a lot, so we better take some extra pack mules. When we finally find their trail, they'll be weeks ahead of us."

"Maybe not." All heads turned to Slim Jim.

"Well?" demanded Gallagher.

"There sure is some sinister thinking going on here. This gang knew every detail down to the time and day the cattle and money would arrive in town. They knew the river is too swollen to cross cattle and the money would have to stay in the bank at least one night. They knew when the sheriff's men would gather for lunch on the west side of the river. They also knew where the marshal's office is and sent men there, and Bo said he was going to send someone to your cabin." Slim Jim paused and laid a gentle hand on Gallagher's shoulder.

"Marshal, he took your wife as a hostage because he knows you. He knows what you're capable of."

Gallagher roughly brushed the man's hand from his shoulder. "So what's your point?" He said it harshly and immediately regretted it, but Slim Jim didn't seem to notice, or he chose not to make an issue of it.

"My point, Marshal, is they've been here for a few days putting all this together. This wasn't an ordinary snatch, grab, and run. This man, Charles Strange, planned this robbery down to the smallest detail. He knew if a posse took after him, they'd sit down over maps first. And I bet he knew we'd come up with the same plan we just did."

"Because it's the only route that makes sense," Gallagher countered. "I still don't see your point."

"My point is, they covered every detail." Slim Jim glanced around. "Except for my son."

"What?"

"Your son?" asked Moses Jackson. "What's he got to do with this?"

"Two days ago, he and his friend came back from fishing the creek where it narrows down in the gorge. And they asked me if they could play on the rope swing hanging from the big pine on the east side of Devil's Peak. You know, where the boulders are closest over the gorge. Of course, I told them Hell no, because it's a two-hundred-foot fall if they miss the boulder. But they told me they saw some men swinging back and forth across the gap. They thought it was funny because one of the men almost fell. Another dropped a whole pack full of supplies down that crevasse."

"Every detail but one," Gallagher repeated thoughtfully. "Let's see that map again." He patted Slim Jim on the back. "Maybe we'll get lucky this time."

"All things being equal, Marshal," the man said. "Victory goes to the lucky."

Gallagher nodded at Slim Jim's wisdom.

The deputy pointed at the crevasse on the map. "I'm guessing they swung across, then stole horses on this side. I'll bet they left them at the gorge and swung back across. Since they likely stashed their own horses and supplies on the other side, they'll have a straight, almost leisurely ride down Buckboard Road to the west, then through this pass all the way to...."

"All of New Mexico or western Colorado."

"While we're following false trails all over the eastern mountains."

"All right," Gallagher said, rolling up the map. "We can't get our horses across the gap, so how do we follow them?"

"We'll have to wait till the river settles down."

"Unacceptable. I'm not going to give them a two- or three-day lead."

Moses Jackson spoke up. "Why don't we build ourselves a raft and rope ourselves across."

"It'll never hold the horses."

"We'll pick up new mounts and packs over on the west side."

Gallagher nodded. "Let's get moving. Time's a-wastin' and we've got a trail to hit."

"Hold on, Derrick," Bo Madison said. "Why don't we cross this afternoon, then eat well and rest up tonight. Hit the trail at first light." He continued without giving Gallagher time to argue. "It's always been the smart thing to do, right? Be rested and get a fresh start. No mistakes that way."

For a moment, Gallagher figured he could take the time to see to his wife's body, but he quickly realized, with a tightening of his chest, he wasn't ready for that task. He had to keep his mind clear and focused. There'd be time to grieve later. He nodded at Bo Madison and looked at the map again. His finger traced along the road and through the pass, then stopped on the last town before a hundred miles of nothing.

"They'll stop here to resupply."

Bo Madison added, "Then that's where we'll greet them." He leaned over the map to see where Gallagher was pointing. "In a little town called Rosebud."

# CHAPTER 4

## ONE DAY PREVIOUS

T HE DAY BEFORE THE SURPRISE shootout with Gallagher's posse, Jay had stopped his horse at the south end of Rosebud and reconsidered Sheriff Travers's invitation to leave and never return. This had been the second time the man had told Jay to leave town at the wrong end of a weapon. The first time was several months ago. When Jay received a request to journey to Texas to assist Melissa-Rae Hampton, the woman whose testimony resulted in his acquittal and the end of his outlaw years, Sheriff Travers told him in no uncertain terms not to return.

Joanne had other intentions, and she'd followed him to Texas. She wouldn't let him stay gone, despite what her father wished, and she had brought him back with her.

With a deep breath, he took stock of the seriousness of the difficult decision he now had to make. If he left this time, Joanne would not follow. He knew this as sure as the sun rose in the east and set in the west. If Jay stayed, while Joanne's father might not actually kill him, the man would most certainly never give his blessings to a marriage between his daughter and a gunfighter-turned-farmer.

Jay started to maneuver his tongue over between two side teeth to wrestle loose the last remnants of smoked turkey and corn from old man Henry's eightieth birthday party. Then he realized he still had a piece of straw stuck in his mouth. He worked the straw around for a while, then slowly arrived at the conclusion to his thinking. He knew what he would do.

He rode off the main path and dismounted in a stand of trees near a creek almost narrow enough to step across. Then he ground-tied his horse and set up camp for the night. He brewed some strong coffee and stared into the fire for long hours until the burning embers simmered away. Then he slept. He would ponder his dilemma in the morning, over another pot of coffee. Only then would he decide how to handle Joanne's father. One thing he knew for sure, he wasn't going to leave the woman he loved.

What seemed like only minutes had passed when the sound of a running horse woke Jay from a deep sleep. As usual, he pulled a gun out of habit, but the horse had not slowed as the rider raced away from town. A quick peek over a bush told Jay the rider was no one he knew. The White horseman—a rarity in Rosebud—didn't notice him.

Rosebud was a true "Colored folks' town." Of the nearly four hundred townsfolk and farmers scattered around the countryside, only one family was White. The town was fairly isolated from the rest of the county and many days passed without a single traveler passing through. That was mainly why Jay was confused. The rider was heading *away* from town so early in the morning and in such a hurry.

Jay dismissed the man from his mind as he turned to prepare his morning coffee. As he sipped the strong, hot liquid, he thought about how to reason with the sheriff. He'd have to approach the task unarmed, of course, so he unbuckled his gun belt. As a farmer who had settled on a patch of land west of town, he had not worn a gun belt nor even carried a pistol tucked into the front of his pants for many months. When the sheriff told him to leave town, all the old habits came rushing back. The first thing he had done was strap on his gun belt and load up his guns.

Jay took one last drink of coffee and tossed the remains of the half-finished pot on the tiny fire. Then he packed his double-gun holster in his saddle pack and gathered up his bedroll. He mounted his horse and rode back through the brush toward the edge of town, although he really hadn't left the town limits the night before.

He chose to enter town by the southern road, not wanting to anger Travers by blatantly riding up the main street. As he approached the warehouse part of town, he watched in curiosity as the same young rider raced his horse back into town, this time riding up one street south of the main street.

Jay frowned. It was almost as if the rider was sneaking around, maybe hiding from someone. The young man jumped from the animal on the run and darted between the general store and the barber shop in a big kind of hurry. He didn't even make the effort to tie his horse properly.

The air was cold at midmorning in early November, and Jay shuddered as a sudden breeze shot through his unbuttoned sheepskin coat. He took another chest full of the crisp air and pulled his hat aside with a swipe of his right hand. He rubbed his left hand through his short hair, then scratched at his itching, four-day-old beard. Suddenly, his destiny was clear to him. If he had to leave Rosebud, he was taking his woman with him. If she stayed, then so would he.

Jay put his hat back on his head and headed toward the general store where he knew the sheriff spent most of his daytime hours. Both Joanne and Mrs. Travers worked at the store. It was very possible he would find all three of them there, and together they would settle the dispute once and for all. Almost as an afterthought, he paused by the young stranger's horse and looked over the man's meager belongings.

His curiosity, Joanne's pa had said, was one of the reasons Jay was always getting involved in trouble. Trouble didn't come looking for him, Travers had said. He went in search of trouble. Jay had argued many times that his curiosity had saved his life, keeping others from getting the drop on him.

"Horse manure," said the sheriff. "Your main problem is you have difficulty keeping your nose out of other people's business."

At the time, Jay had no argument. He knew the lawman's words were closer to the truth than he was willing to admit. Just as true was the impossibility of trying to change a decade of habits in only a few months.

Jay was about to ride on when something out of the ordinary caught his glance. He leaned over and tugged at a bit of hair sticking out of the man's saddle pocket. It came free and Jay yanked his hand back in horror as the hair and the scalp it was attached to fell into the dirt street. He slid from his saddle, retrieved the scalp, and examined it, finally coming to the conclusion it had once belonged to the child of one of the nearby native tribes.

Jay further examined the stranger's packs and found several more scalps. He recognized some of the tribal ornaments in the hair and was shocked to discover the scalps were from all ages of men, women, and children. Disturbingly, none of the scalps were from hunters or warriors, but only from tribes Jay knew to be peaceful and nomadic. Then he found two blond scalps and one from someone who'd had long, straight brown hair.

Suddenly alert, Jay mentally welcomed his old friend and shadow, trouble. The young stranger had left his horse in front of a feed store closed for the weekend. Other shops and barns all along the street, normally bustling with activity during the week, were also closed at the early hour. Whatever the young rider wanted, he was going about it mighty suspiciously.

Jay grabbed two guns from his saddle pack, checked them by habit, and tucked both into the front of his pants, butts pointed outward for the easy draw. He started to unpack his holster as well, but hesitated. If this turned out to be a misunderstanding, riding in armed to the teeth wouldn't help his case with his future father-in-law.

In search of the young rider, he trotted through the gap to the next street, with the general store to his right and the barbershop to his left. When he reached the boardwalk, he saw the confrontation out in the street.

There were seven riders facing Joanne's father. Though Sheriff Travers held a Winchester cradled across his left arm, right index finger in the trigger guard, Jay could see the concern etched into the dark features of his face. Gray hair peeked from under the wide-brimmed, beige hat sitting low on the sheriff's forehead.

Facing him, the leader of the group sat unconcerned on his mount, chewing tobacco, and occasionally spitting brown juice near the sheriff's boots. He was a big man with broad shoulders and shoulder-length, brown hair, and he wore only a shirt in the freezing air. Hanging from the back of the man's saddle were several ropes holding a dozen scalps each. Most were adorned with items of different Indian tribal origins, but there was an occasional ribbon bow and rawhide tieback so popular south of the border. Jay had the feeling this was not a man to trifle with.

Travers and the big man bantered back and forth about dinner and drinking, then Travers launched into his ritualistic speech about not wearing guns in town.

Possession of guns was the dominant point of contention between Jay and the sheriff. Even when Jay finally packed his guns away, Joanne's father was not happy because he was certain Jay would eventually and inevitably once again follow the path of the gun. As the sheriff said, it was in his blood. He could only pretend to be a farmer. At the core of his soul, he was and always would be a gunfighter. Over the months, the dispute had evolved into a power struggle for Travers and an independence struggle for Jay. But deep inside, Jay had a feeling the sheriff was not far from wrong.

He was what he was. He'd been that way for over ten years. Would another ten years change him?

The leader of the newcomers paid Travers no mind after his speech. He just laughed off the gun law and spat more juice, this time landing a fat splatter against the sheriff's pant leg, near his ankle. Jay couldn't hear all of the exchange, but he caught some words about eight to one odds not favoring the lawman.

Jay took two steps up onto the boardwalk, just about to speak to better odds, when he froze at the sound of a gun hammer clicking close beside him. A shuffle of feet drew his gaze to the doorway of the general store, and he saw his beautiful Joanne standing in the grip of the horseman he had seen earlier. The man held a gun to her head.

# CHAPTER 5

THE MAN NUDGED JOANNE OUT farther from the doorway. Jay didn't make any sudden moves.

"Hey, Hank," called the leader without taking his eyes off the sheriff. "You got that under control over there?"

Hank chuckled with a cocky sneer and tightened his arm around Joanne's neck. He forced her head back against his shoulder.

"I believe I do, Mr. Strange," he replied.

Jay's eyes narrowed at the familiar name. *Strange?*

He looked over at the leader's collection of scalps again and a shudder raced down his spine. He had heard of a ruthless gang known as the Strange Scalpers. It might have seemed a silly name for a gang of roughriders had he not known of the gang's namesake and leader, Charles Strange. It was said he terrorized the frontier—killing, looting, and taking scalps for no reason other than because he could.

Seeing Strange in person convinced Jay there was nothing humorous about these men. The man on the lead horse was supremely confident, even cocky. The young horseman Jay had seen obviously surveyed the town earlier in the morning and reported back. Strange had a plan and the situation was totally under his control. Jay could not believe it was only coincidence Hank had grabbed the lawman's daughter as a hostage.

That conclusion unsettled Jay. It seemed Charles Strange had everything planned out. He had confronted the sheriff just after Travers visited with his wife or daughter at the general store. He had accounted for every detail, except possibly one. He hadn't accounted for Jay.

Hank interrupted his thoughts. "Why don't you just lay them irons down real careful like, mister."

"Can't do that," Jay said quietly.

"No? Well, maybe you want me to splatter this woman's brains all over the wall here. You really want to take that chance?"

"I reckon I'm gonna have to," Jay said. "Knowing who you all are, I figure you're going to kill her anyway. So I have to try to save her life."

Jay didn't look Joanne in the eye. He didn't want to see her fear. He knew he had carelessly walked into the fray without checking his cover. He'd been easily outflanked because of his carelessness, and now his woman was a hostage. He had only one chance to save her, and it depended entirely on Joanne. She'd seen him in action in Texas. She knew what he could do.

*But would she know what she had to do? And would she know the right moment to do it?*

"Go 'head and try, mister."

Hank hugged Joanne closer to him and tightened his grip on his gun, pressing its barrel harder against her temple. He said the last part a bit too loud and too high-pitched. Jay knew the man would be figuring Jay was either crazy or confident. Either way, he was beginning to feel the fear. Jay decided to make the man sweat a bit as he noticed Charles Strange focus his attention on him.

"Caruthers, cover the sheriff."

A man moved his horse up from the rear and aimed his shotgun at the lawman while Charles Strange moved his horse closer to Jay.

"You got guts, mister," he said.

"So do you." Jay decided to match the man's confidence. Maybe there was an advantage to be gained in unnerving him. Staring into Strange's brown eyes, he knew the man wouldn't make a move until he was sure he understood and controlled the new and unexpected development in his plan. "And so does Hank."

"Yeah, well, I know empty bravado when I hear it." Strange pondered him for a moment. "The way I see things, I have a decided advantage. I can assure you *my* bravado is not empty."

He ended his remark with a chuckle, but Jay simply gave the man his emptiest deadpan gaze. Charles Strange cocked his head.

"You know who I am," he said. It was not a question.

"I've heard talk," Jay said.

"Then you know what I'm capable of. Are you willing to take the chance of innocent men and women getting killed?"

"From what I've heard, you take scalps and leave dead bodies in every town you visit. The way I figure it, this visit is no different. The only question in my mind is how many of your men are you willing to lose also."

Strange chuckled casually again and shook his head. "All we want is a little money." He nodded over his left shoulder to where the small bank stood next door to the sheriff's office. "And maybe some free supplies and meals for my men."

"If we agree to all of that, will you leave without causing any more trouble?"

Strange made a snorting sound. "That's not how we play the game."

In that statement, Jay knew there was absolutely no chance of talking his way out of this predicament. It was in the man's eyes. He had to *take* what he wanted. If something was given to him freely, he didn't want it. He wasn't here for money or supplies or food, though in the end he might take all he wanted. He was here to play his game of terror.

"I understand people are going to get hurt," Jay said. "But your men are going to be among them."

Strange snorted. "You know, I've never actually seen a Negro town." He looked around. "Maybe we'll just start ourselves a Negro fire and burn this place down and everybody who lives here. Except her." Strange nodded at Joanne. "Maybe we'll carry your Black bitch off with us and have some fun with her." He paused. "*All* of us."

Jay shook his head. "Only some of you will live long enough to have any kind of fun. The rest of you will be dead."

"You play a dangerous game, with bad odds."

Jay formed a half-smile that never quite reached his eyes. "That's because you don't know what *I'm* capable of."

Strange's eyebrows went up in mock surprise. "Well, enlighten me. I'm growing weary of this conversation."

Jay paused for a few seconds. "Ever heard of Jason Peares?"

Strange's left eye twitched, but that was all the reaction he showed. It was enough.

"Well, I've always wanted to meet you."

"It's your lucky day," Jay said without emotion. "You seem to like games, Mr. Strange. How about a numbers game? Instead of eight to two, what if the odds were only three against two before your guys even got a shot off?"

"So, you've got guts *and* an imagination. I'm curious how you figure three to two odds. I'm still seeing eight to two, which is only slightly better than eight to one."

Jay nodded. "The one you called Caruthers over there. Well, he really isn't ready for shootin' action." Jay paused as the realization fell over Strange's countenance. "His shotgun is loaded, but he hasn't pulled his hammers back. In the time it takes him to thumb one hammer, he'll get my first bullet. And your hands aren't even close to your gun. You'll be dead before you even clear leather. And, seein' as you're sitting right between me and them, I figure they won't shoot at me for fear of hitting you. I'll get one more of them and the sheriff will get at least one more." Jay shrugged. "So we're really looking at three against two after that."

Charles Strange's smile disappeared only for a moment. "You're forgettin' about Hank here. That would make it four to two if I were inclined to play along with your little fantasy. And there's the little detail with the lady. You know...*the one with the gun at her head.*"

"Hell, if I'm Hank, I've got to be doing some serious thinking right about now, and I'd be feeling pretty damned useless. If he shoots the woman, I'm going to shoot him dead on the spot. He won't even get a chance to think about a second shot.

"Or, if he tries to shoot me first, you know, if his gun's no longer at her head," Jay shrugged, trying to sound as relaxed as Strange seemed to be, "well, I'm still gonna shoot him. So really, she's the only thing keeping Hank alive.

"In fact," Jay paused and looked over at Hank, cutting straight through to his very soul with his penetrating gaze, "I'm just waiting for Hank to blink so I can put a bullet right between his eyes."

Strange grunted. "Have you ever seen what happens when you shoot somebody in the head? Their whole body jerks in contraction because death takes a few seconds to take hold. Shootin' him is just gonna cause him to shoot her."

"Maybe," Jay said, still gazing intently at Hank. "But a wise man once said there's a little spot right between the eyes and about an inch above the eyebrows. If you shoot a person there, the bullet blows through the part of the brain that controls every muscle in the body and the whole body just relaxes. And Hank's starting to sweat. I think he believes I can do it."

Jay flicked his gaze to Joanne quickly and twitched the corner of his mouth, a partial gesture of confidence. She moved almost imperceptibly, barely half an inch. She turned her gaze a bit to the right, jogging her head to the side.

With that tiny movement, Jay saw both of Hank's eyes. He pulled his belt gun and fired in one smooth motion. The loud clapping sound of the shot underscored the violence of the man's death. Eyes open, the man never realized when his life ended. He may have seen the blurred movement of Jay's arm, may have seen the flash of exploding gunpowder from the barrel of Jay's gun. The slightest fraction of time later, a neat bullet hole appeared in Hank's forehead, and he was dead.

The back of Hank's skull exploded gore onto the wall behind him as Jay's bullet ripped through his head. The instant his brain was blown apart, Hank gasped a final soft sigh, and his entire body collapsed like a rag doll.

Jay turned his attention to the rest of the Strange Scalpers. He pulled his second gun from his belt and began shooting even before Hank's body crumbled to the ground. His second shot caved in the side of Caruthers's head, even as the man thumbed his shotgun. Sheriff Travers's rifle barked, and another man fell. Jay tried to get a shot off at Strange, but the man reared his horse and charged. Jay dodged to the side as the man crashed his horse up onto the boardwalk and raced through the general store window.

Jay looked for more targets, but the Scalpers gang was scattering everywhere. Just as suddenly as it had begun, the gunfight was over.

Hank and Caruthers were dead, but the man Sheriff Travers shot was only wounded and managed to ride away with the others. Charles Strange had escaped through the general store, wrecking it on his way out the back door.

As Travers looked over toward his daughter on the boardwalk, Jay stepped close to Joanne and touched the side of her face. She trembled and gripped his hand tightly. She stared at him, but he saw no anger in her eyes. Instead, he saw a primal fear, and he could tell she was looking to him for answers he could not provide. There was no reason or explanation for the actions of men like the Strange Scalpers.

He wrapped his arms around her shoulders and held her close. After a few minutes, she nodded and stepped from his embrace. She kissed the inside of his palm, and a silent moment bonded them more deeply than words ever could. He felt the strength of love as he had never felt it before. Earlier, he had come so close to leaving her—a mistake he never would make again.

As he turned and walked out into the middle of the street, he knew he and the sheriff would have to come up with a plan to deal with Strange's return. Jay knew the man's type. He would have revenge on his mind. Pursuit by posse would be best, but

Rosebud was short on that particular skill, and soliciting a posse from the county seat way over east of the mountains would take far too long.

Jay spoke with Sheriff Travers as two boys started dragging the bodies away. Joanne joined Jay and her father in the street, but their conversation was interrupted by the warning shout from the east end of the street. More riders were coming.

Gallagher and his posse rode confidently, weapons at the ready. Their prey's tracks were fresh, at best only an hour old. He had hoped to beat the murderers to town, but at least there was no indication Strange knew he was being followed. If true, even though the man believed he had outwitted a posse, it was a serious lapse of judgment. A critical error Gallagher found hard to believe a man like Charles Strange would make. He didn't want to believe such a careful planner would be so overconfident, but that clearly seemed to be the case.

If the roles were reversed, Gallagher wouldn't make that kind of assumption. Either Strange wasn't as smart as he seemed, or he was leading Gallagher's posse into an ambush. Gallagher was prepared for both possibilities.

His men were spread into an inverted V with Gallagher and Bo Madison leading side by side at the point. Gallagher glanced at his friend to his left, shotgun in his right grip and rifle in his left. Madison wore no hat despite the chill. He kept his scalp completely clean-shaven except for the stripe of graying hair on top of his head and down the back of his neck.

Gallagher remembered back over the past twenty years. Madison had always prepared for the hunt by shaving his head with a sinister-looking Mohawk. He now looked as mean and dangerous at fifty-five as he had at thirty-five. Few men ever made the mistake of calling that man an old-timer.

With four men on their left flank and three on their right, Gallagher and Madison rode slowly up the center of the main street of Rosebud. The marshal studied the dark faces peering at him and his men from the boardwalk. He saw wariness and suspicion, so he smiled and nodded at some. He didn't want to appear threatening.

He saw something more also. He saw concern and fear on many of the faces. Something had happened here. Had the Strange Scalpers already visited?

Whatever had happened, he knew the danger was past. Otherwise, the people would not be milling about outside.

Gallagher was scanning the shops and other buildings along the street when Madison directed his attention to the dead bodies. One man lay on the boardwalk covered by a coat, while the other lay in the middle of the street. Two boys had just picked up this man's legs and were dragging him away.

From the distance, Gallagher noticed the Black sheriff talking to another man in the street where the body had been. The other man glanced briefly toward the posse, then turned back to his conversation as if he had no concern for them. The man had seen the posse's clearly visible badges and was not bothered, so Gallagher concluded these men were not a threat.

He watched a very attractive, slender, dark-skinned woman join the two men in the street. She hugged the one man and conversed with the sheriff. Then she looked over at the posse with a confused expression, and Gallagher realized the lawman was staring at Bo Madison. Gallagher glanced over to his left and saw Madison staring wide-eyed at the sheriff.

"Bo? What is it?"

"It's him!"

In almost slow motion, the other man's head came around as Madison's weapons came down to bear on him. Gallagher looked back at the man standing with the sheriff, finally seeing the side of his face as he turned. His familiar face exploded from the past.

As the man turned, Gallagher saw he wore two guns tucked into his belt. Suddenly, everything about the man was familiar. He had the same tall, slender physique and the same light brown complexion he remembered from ten years past. The same light brown eyes with the penetrating gaze that seemed to bore right into his very soul. He looked more seasoned and battle-hardened than the last time the two had crossed paths. His face was leaner and held harder features. Slight crow's feet framed his eyes now. Those penetrating brown eyes seemed more intelligent and observant than before—less reckless. But the gunfighter was no less hesitant.

Gallagher gasped as recognition and hatred blazed through the man's eyes. His own breath caught in his throat and his own hatred boiled quickly to the surface as he faced Jason Peares.

The outlaw who killed my son!

Then Gallagher did something he had never done in his entire professional life. He collared his instinct to attack. There were civilians all around—too close to the target. For the first time in his life, he froze.

Bo Madison did not.

# CHAPTER 6

B Y THE TIME GALLAGHER FINALLY reacted, nearly a full second had passed. As he tried to make his body move and do something, anything, a part of his brain recognized he was in a panicked space of super-slow-motion reality. His eyes darted back and forth as his vision cataloged who was shooting whom. It was almost as if he wasn't really there. He felt like a spectator, watching the gunfight in relative safety from beside the road. Yet, he realized in the normal passage of time everything had happened so quickly. Wild bullets flew, and people died. A little girl on the boardwalk was dead, the woman and the sheriff were down, Madison was hit, and someone in his posse behind him cried out in pain. Even Jason Peares was falling but still shooting.

Gallagher careened his horse around and hollered for withdrawal. His posse could easily have won the gunfight, and they would have too, in a few more seconds. But the screams and cries of the innocent bystanders cut into his heart. More innocent people would die if he stayed to win the fight.

He was so intent on finding the Strange Scalpers, he'd let his guard down and wasn't prepared for any other threat, even the surprise of seeing Jason Peares. The situation had quickly exploded out of control. As he and his men raced out of town, he saw Matthew McDonnell riding alongside Madison's horse, keeping the big man from falling out of his saddle. A final shot echoed up the street and the top of McDonnell's head exploded in a gush of red gore. He fell over sideways, dragging Bo Madison down with him.

Wincing in pain, Jay tried and failed to roll onto his side. Before he opened his eyes, a flood of cries and screams invaded his ears.

*There's no more gunfire, but who's dead and who's alive? Where is Joanne? And what had happened to the man who hated him with every fiber of his being, hated him enough to shoot up a street full of innocent people?*

He had seen the eyes, had drawn a straight bead on the face. He could have ended the ten-year hunt right then.

*If only I'd reloaded my guns.*

Jay knew Marshal Gallagher would be back. He would re-group after he attended to his wounded. Then he would return. Jay recalled the man's words from ten years back. He had heard them with his own ears.

Gallagher had put his posse up at the very same hotel a much younger Jason Peares had checked into. The only miracle that saved his life back then was because the hotel owner's son had relieved his father for a short time just before Jay checked in. The father knew Gallagher was hunting the outlaw, but the son did not. So the father didn't know Jay was in the hotel.

He and Gallagher had stayed in upstairs rooms next door to each other, but Gallagher never knew. The young Jason Peares had listened to the angry conversation through the wall.

"He killed my only son, Bo! I'll hunt that murdering son of a bitch to the sands of both oceans until I find him. There's no-where he can hide. I don't care if it takes a whole year, or ten, or twenty, or *fifty* years. I'll find him someday. You hear me? And when I find him, I'll shoot him dead! There'll be no words, no questions, and no explanations. I don't care if he's old and gray or crippled or a reformed preacher man. He's a *dead man,* Bo! That I promise."

*None of it made sense,* Jay thought as he sucked in a deep breath to steel himself against the pain flooding his body. *Why now after ten whole years? Did news of my involvement in that mess with the cattle baron, Pritchett, down in Texas travel far enough to put the vengeful lawman back on my trail? Or did they finally track me down after that business with the Sadler brothers and Melissa-Rae Hampton?*

Maybe word had gotten to him from Major Clark, who commanded the Buffalo Soldiers of the Ninth Cavalry. The major had asked for his references before hiring him to scout for them and, as evidence of his skills on the trail, he'd told the major he had eluded Marshal Gallagher for two years.

None of that explained why they had ridden into town so obviously unprepared. The Black man, Bo Madison, Jay recalled, seemed surprised to see him. Clearly the posse was on his trail, but it was almost as if they didn't expect to find him in Rosebud. It just didn't make sense until he considered the possibility that perhaps someone had told them he was last seen in Rosebud. Maybe they simply came here to start their search, to find out where he'd gone next.

Jay's purpose was clear. Now that the marshal knew where Jay was, he'd return unless Jay found him first. Jay knew he had to obey the same rules as Gallagher. No words. No questions. No explanations. He would find them and kill them before they killed him or anyone else close to him.

With great effort, Jay opened his eyes. At first, he wasn't sure what he was looking at. The world was blurry. Then the panic set in.

*What if I've been shot in the eyes?*

He took another breath to calm the fear, then blinked several times to clear away the tears of pain. He heard sounds to his right and moved his head carefully. He saw the sheriff, and his breath choked in his throat. The man's bloody body lay beside him in the street. Jay rolled to his knees, hollering in pain with the effort. Finally, he knelt beside the sheriff.

"Travers!" Jay grabbed at the man's bloody shirt and shook

him gently, but the lawman didn't move. He shook the man again.

"Sheriff, get up! You can't die. Not you." He gazed down at the man's still body. The right side of his face was blown away, leaving only a mass of blood and hanging flesh. He also had taken a full shotgun blast high in the left side of his chest, another rifle shot in the stomach, and one in the upper thigh of his right leg.

Rough hands shoved Jay away from the sheriff's body, and a doctor and his assistant knelt beside him. Jay heard a wail behind him, interrupted by violent coughing. Then he saw Joanne holding a young girl in her lap. Blood soaked Joanne's coat near the right shoulder. She'd been shot but didn't seem to notice. The girl in her lap had been shot in the neck. Even as he watched, the girl clutched Joanne's arm so tightly she winced. Another scream erupted from the girl as her body convulsed one last time before she was silent and still.

Jay sat frozen in shock, unable to move. Then he began to tremble. He couldn't stop it— couldn't control it. Life had been so peaceful for six months since he and Joanne had returned from Texas.

*How could this have happened? How could lawmen simply ride into town and start shooting? Where was this manhunter's reputed honor?*

Jay had kept tabs on the marshal for the first few years after his narrow escape from the posse. The man's professionalism was uncompromised. Had the years of desire for revenge turned him into a raging animal no better than the Strange Scalpers?

A long wail of anguish from the general store startled him as he sat on his rump. As he looked over, he saw the elderly Mrs. Gates sitting on the boardwalk, cradling her husband in her lap. Jay realized the store owner must have caught a stray bullet from Gallagher's posse, remembering he'd stepped through the doorway after the shootout with Charles Strange.

Jay clutched his stomach, then his chest. He tried to press the pain away but realized it wasn't a physical pain that was crippling him. This was his fault. He should have left when the sheriff told him to.

When he realized he couldn't make the pain go away, he buried his face in his hands against his knees and just rocked forward and back. He heard Joanne's voice beside him, above him, felt her hands on his shoulders. He looked up, but then she was gone.

Through cloudy eyes, he saw her kneel beside her father. Mrs. Travers knelt beside her. They hugged and sobbed together, trying to comfort each other. When Mrs. Travers looked over toward Jay, he couldn't bear the blame he saw in her gaze. He turned away and painfully hauled himself to his feet.

Jay stared down the empty street where the posse had ridden away. He stifled back the panic and the pain, but he felt a frigid cold creep along his bones until his insides were filled with an icy hatred. He felt the long, lonely road calling to him again. This time, he would not be on the run. This time, he would be the hunter. He would serve up his own brand of justice for heartless men who would shoot down innocent women and children to satisfy their lust for revenge.

"There's nowhere to run, Gallagher!" he called to the empty street. "Nowhere! I'll find you!"

He grunted as he bent down to retrieve his hat then squashed it angrily on his head.

"You hear me, Gallagher! I'll find you!" He shouted at the top of his voice, immune to the people standing around staring at him like he was a crazed lunatic. "I'll kill your whole posse. I'll find your families, and I'll kill them too. Then I'll cut you open and tear your heart out!"

He paused breathlessly, chest heaving, body trembling. Then he looked down at Joanne and her mother, but they just stared at him like they didn't know him. He started to turn away but instead, looked down at the sheriff. After a brief moment, he collected his weapons and walked up the street.

"I'll kill them all."

Gallagher looked around at the shocked faces of his men after they brought their horses to a stop.

"My God, Marshal. What have we done?"

Gallagher just shook his head as he dismounted. "Slim, cover our trail."

Slim Jim rode back a ways and dismounted. He found a perch among the rocks and aimed his sniper rifle back along the trail. The other members of the posse gathered around Gallagher. He took a deep breath and removed his hat, then wiped sweat from his brow with the back of his sleeve.

"He'll be coming, Marshal," Pickens said. "We'd best get prepared."

"Naw," Billy Hutchinson countered. "He got shot. I saw him go down."

"Don't matter." Pickens spat in disgust. "We all know Jason Peares. Shot or not, he'll ride as soon as he's able."

"I agree," added Moses Jackson. "He'll figure we're hunting him again. All those people we killed.... Damn!"

"That was an accident," Robert Hutchinson said.

"Tell that to Jason Peares."

Gallagher looked up at his men still mounted and started to speak.

Willie Smith interrupted. "Marshal, we've got to go back and get our boys."

"They're dead, Willie."

Robert Hutchinson added, "We don't know that for sure, Marshal. We can't leave them out there."

"They're dead! I know it because I saw it."

Gallagher replayed the brutal scene still fresh in his memory. Even as Jason Peares was turning toward the posse, Bo Madison was aiming his weapons. As soon as the gunfighter recognized Gallagher, he drew both of the guns stuck in his belt at the same time. Jason Peares had snapped off three quick shots at Bo with one gun before Madison even pulled his trigger the first time, and Bo had his weapons already pointed at the gunfighter! Then the gunman had his other gun centered right in the middle of Gallagher's chest.

*Christ, I've never seen anyone draw so fast!*

Gallagher had tensed, but for some unexplainable reason the gun aimed at him had been empty. The right gun wasn't. Gallagher remembered hearing two bullets thump into Bo Madison's chest split seconds before the sound of the gunshots reached his ears. Bo gasped in pain and jerked in reaction. His left arm was knocked to the side and the rifle went off. A little girl screamed and fell on the boardwalk. The shotgun in Bo's right hand continued its journey downward and both barrels exploded almost at the same time, catching the sheriff full in the face and chest. Even as the sheriff fell, his own rifle fired into the woman next to Jay. She screamed and went down.

Others in the posse behind Gallagher started shooting as well. Jason caught two bullets, and he too went down, still shooting. Madison's head snapped back as Jay's last shot struck him in the top of his head, splattering bone and blood into the air.

It had all happened in the space of only one or two seconds of time. The result was five people dead or wounded. McDonnell hadn't even known Bo Madison was already dead as he rode up to guide his horse and hold him in the saddle. That was when the gunfighter had scored a lucky shot to the back of McDonnell's head.

*No,* Gallagher thought. *Knowing Jason Peares, his shot was anything but lucky.* In frustration, Gallagher pounded his fists against his saddle. His horse whinnied in protest.

"He wasn't supposed to be there!"

"There were accidental deaths on both sides." Moses Jackson summarized their plight. "But he's gonna remember what you said ten years ago, Marshal. He'll be coming."

"So what are we going to do about him?" Pickens asked. "And what do we do about the Strange Scalpers? We can't take them both on."

Gallagher reacted as if punched when he suddenly remembered why they were on the trail in the first place.

"We didn't come here to pick a fight with Jason Peares. We're here to bring those murdering bastards to justice. And that's *all* we're going to do."

"Just for argument's sake," Jackson said. "Let's assume Jason Peares ain't likely to share our point of view."

"We'll avoid him," Gallagher said. "If he comes after us, we'll try to reason with him. If he doesn't want to be reasonable, *then* we'll kill him."

The men looked around at each other. Again, Moses Jackson spoke for the group.

"Marshal, you got a good look at him back there. We all did." He paused. "This ain't the same reckless, twenty-year-old kid with a fast gun we chased ten years ago. He's a battle-hardened veteran, a seasoned gunfighter now. We've all heard about him over the years. He's faced the worst kind of life this frontier can throw at a man, and he's survived. Hell, he survived us."

"Listen up, all of you," Gallagher said, looking around at the posse. "I know what you're thinking. We're old. We're slow. Maybe it's gettin' about time to retire. Hell, I've got creaking bones just like the rest of you, and I've eaten a bit too much over the years too." He patted his gut.

"But we have a responsibility to uphold the law and protect the citizens of our town, as well as those beyond our town if we have to. It's our job to protect those who can't protect themselves, especially against terrorizers like the Scalpers. We have a responsibility to serve justice to those who violate the law. We've had every bit as hard a life as anyone else, including Jason Peares, and we have survived. We've survived because we are the best. Even at our age, no other posse in this whole blessed country has accomplished half of what we have. With one exception, we've always brought our man in.

"We're not after Jason Peares." Gallagher took a deep breath. "But I'll tell you this—if he gets in our way, we'll deal with him. There's never been or never will there be a finer group of men

I'd want to call my posse. I'm proud to ride with any of you, no matter what the odds or the situation."

"Maybe he won't listen, but someone else in Rosebud might," Moses Jackson said. "Maybe he's got some kinfolk we can reason with. Persuade them to get a message to him, and maybe we can end this before it gets out of hand."

Gallagher lowered his gaze and shook his head. "It's already out of hand." Still, he thought about Moses's suggestion. "But your idea surely makes sense. Who would ride back there?"

"It's my idea. I'll do it. Although, I'll probably ride around up the south road to town, so I don't cross his path if he's tracking us. It'll take a couple of hours extra, but if it gets him off our back it'll be worth it."

"All right, deliver your message to anyone who'll listen. Then get back on the trail. My guess is we'll be trailing Charles Strange straight down to the New Mexico border. You can catch up with us there." Gallagher shook Moses's hand, and the man rode off.

"Watch your back!" Billy Hutchinson hollered after him.

"Watch your front too!" his brother added.

Gallagher looked each man in the eye. "Shall we ride?"

"Hell, yes!"

# CHAPTER 7

THERE WERE TWO MAIN TRAILS leading to Rosebud. One led in from the east, and the other led in from the south. The wagon trail out to the west connected the town with homesteads dotting the neighboring hills and valleys. Jay's one-room shack was about fifteen minutes by horse, outside the western edge of town. He lived in what used to be a tool shed on one of the larger farms.

Jay took shots to his inner left thigh, his right arm near the shoulder, and the muscle just under his right armpit. Two were just creases. Only the shoulder wound had penetrated the skin. They were all minor flesh wounds, but they still hurt like hell. It took Jay slightly more than three hours to treat his superficial wounds and pack his trail supplies. Then he headed back to town, riding up the minor street north of the main street. Joanne stood with her mother outside the doctor's clinic. As he drew up, he could see both women had been crying. Joanne started toward Jay's horse, but Mrs. Travers held her back with a gentle hand and said something. Joanne nodded and went back inside the clinic.

Jay said nothing as Mrs. Travers approached his horse carrying a small pack. He steeled himself against the onslaught of words of blame and guilt he knew were coming. She started to speak, but Jay waved her quiet with a single movement of his hand.

"I know you blame me for getting your husband killed, but

I'm not going to leave my woman, Mrs. Travers. There's nothing you can say to change my mind, so don't waste your words."

"I had no such words for you, young man. I saw what those lawmen did. They drew first. I know it wasn't your fault."

"But it was."

"What do you mean?"

"That marshal blames me for his son's death. He swore he would hunt me until the end of time." Jay couldn't hold her gaze. "I reckon this was his day."

"So your past has caught up to you again. Just like last year."

He nodded.

"And now you're leaving again. Do you know what this is doing to my daughter?"

"I'm not leaving her. I'm going to find those men. I'm through running."

She repeated her question more forcefully. "Do you *realize* what you're putting her through?"

"Marshal Gallagher is one of the deadliest manhunters I've ever crossed paths with, Mrs. Travers. If I don't go after him, he'll come after me. I ran from him and his men for almost two years before I finally lost them. He'll never quit now. He knows where I live. If I don't go find him now, more people will get hurt when he returns for me."

"Jay, I know you love Joanne. And she truly loves you. But how many other people are looking for you because of your past?"

Jay stared at her for a moment then looked away. "I don't know."

She stepped closer and touched his hand gently. "You're a good man, Jay. One I'd be proud to call my son. But maybe you should be thinking about people other than yourself." She hesitated. "Think about the pain you'd bring to your wife and family years from now if someone else comes for you. And what if they found you? Think about what you'd be asking Joanne to endure."

She offered him the small pack. "Here's extra water, clean rags, and some medicine for your wounds."

Jay brushed the pack aside. "I just have flesh wounds. I'll get by." He started to move his horse away, but Mrs. Travers grabbed his reins.

"You always were too damned stubborn for your own good. Just like my husband. You're going on the trail and your wounds will get infected if you don't care for them properly. I did some nursing in my younger days, so do what I tell you."

He nodded. "Yes, ma'am."

"Change your wounds with clean rags every day and wash the old rags in boiling water before using them again. Wipe the wounds with this." She opened the pack and held up a small vial of liquid. "If the wounds get puffy or swollen, then you'll have to drink some of this. A little bit every day." She held up another small bottle.

"Yes, ma'am." She squeezed his hand, and he took the pack from her. After he stashed it in a pocket behind his saddle, he tipped his hat and kicked his horse into motion.

"Jay," she called after him. He stopped and turned in the saddle. "He's alive."

"What? Who?"

"My husband. He's still alive but just barely."

For a moment, Jay was unable to speak. Finally, he found his voice. "Can I see him?"

She shook her head. "He needs his rest. Before you come back, I want you to think about my daughter." Mrs. Travers paused. "Think about what's best for her."

He nodded, but she continued.

"And if you don't return, then I'll know you've decided to do the right thing."

She turned away, and Jay watched her walk back toward the doctor's office. Shocked, he simply sat there on his horse. Mrs. Travers had been on his side every time her husband lit into him about his outlaw and gunfighter days. Except for Joanne, he was now without allies in the family.

*How long before Joanne also chooses common sense over love? What really is the right thing to do? Take a chance on love or abandon love to spare Joanne the possibility of future pain?*

Mrs. Travers turned in the doorway and hollered at him. "And don't you go killing those men's families. Their kin had nothing to do with this."

Jay nodded and spurred his horse into motion. He turned his attention to his task as manhunter. He really had no intention of hunting and killing the families of Gallagher's men. He had been out of his mind with rage after seeing Sheriff Travers's body and those of the other innocent victims.

As he rode, he considered his predicament. Clearly, Marshal Gallagher and his posse had not expected to find him in Rosebud. The smart thing would be to ride the trail hard again, away from the posse. It was what he had always done before when Gallagher, or any other manhunter, was on his trail. He always tried to lose his pursuers and avoid a deadly confrontation, but he couldn't do that this time.

From their encounter, he knew they would conclude he now lived in, or close to, Rosebud. If they figured he'd settled down, perhaps made a family, they'd know he could not just pack up and run again. Life was a lot different at thirty years old than at twenty. A man was usually a lot more settled. He'd have to defend his homestead and family. Since the hunters now knew where he lived, they could make him sweat. They could make him go insane wondering when they'd return for him. He had to hunt them down and kill them first.

Jay nodded to himself as he approached the east end of town. That would be their reasoning too. And he would oblige them, but only to a point. They'd know he was coming for them, so he would go. They'd run for a while, then they'd try to bait him, lie in wait, and set a trap. He intended to make sure they were disappointed.

He would follow them from a distance—never showing himself, perhaps harassing them until they tired of running. He would make them sweat, then he would draw them into his trap.

He'd make them hunt him again. When they did, he would be waiting.

Suddenly, Jay reined his horse to a stop. Just as Charles Strange sent a man into town on the southern trail, it would be child's play for Marshal Gallagher to figure out the same tactic. They wouldn't run for long, and there was nothing to stop part of the posse from backtracking along the southern route to get back into town. They'd either take hostages or they'd swing in behind him while he was trailing the rest of the posse. They'd probably try to sandwich him on the trail from the front and back. Jay recalled some of Gallagher's tactics ten years before. Always when he thought he was safe, the posse turned up right behind him.

Gallagher was a wily and crafty manhunter. Almost four hours had passed since the shootout, and Gallagher's men would be perhaps four or five miles along the eastern route which turned south. They'd had plenty time enough for them to regroup and figure out another strategy. Jay turned his horse and raced back through town, down the southern trail to hunt his hunters. His first hunt was short-lived. He was barely a mile south of town when he saw the rider.

The land south of Rosebud was mostly flat, then turned hilly as the road veered to the west. The rider rounded the last hill and came into plain sight as Jay calmly pulled his Spencer rifle from its scabbard. It was specially modified with an extra-long, forty-four-inch, octagonal barrel and had a single-shot chamber. It also featured a four-power spyglass affixed to the barrel where the metal sighting tab would normally be. At just under half a mile away, the approaching rider wouldn't even be a challenge to hit.

Jay slid painfully from his mount, perched the long rifle across his saddle, and brought the rider into focus. As he expected, he recognized the rider as one of Gallagher's posse—the dark-skinned man with short, knotty-looking, gray hair. One of the original posse members from ten years ago. Moses Jackson was his name.

He'd had many opportunities to learn all their names. Gallagher's posse was famous across the northwest and southwest, and everyone knew of them and talked about them. Jay had certainly been close enough to them back then to easily recognize any of them. He'd even managed to kill one of them during a chase across the rocky flats of southern Utah.

The crosshairs of the spyglass centered on the man's chest even as Moses Jackson slowed his horse to a stop. Jay watched the magnified image of the man pull out his own spyglass, then saw the man's expression change from surprise to horror. Jay pulled the trigger as Moses Jackson spurred his horse into motion.

Jay used special handmade, .50-caliber cartridges for his Spencer. The seven-hundred-grain bullet was propelled by the explosion of one hundred seventy grains of black powder. Under most conditions, such a bullet could punch a hole clean through his target, and whoever or whatever was unfortunate enough to be in the way, front or back, man or horse.

The recoil of the powerful shot hammered straight into the bandaged wound under Jay's right armpit. He grimaced and almost dropped the rifle. By the time he recovered from the numbing pain, the other horse was almost on top of him. Jay pulled his left gun and took aim. Then he realized the horse had no rider. He gazed off into the distance and saw a crumpled form lying on the ground. He had not missed.

Jay holstered his gun and packed away his long rifle, then climbed back onto his horse. A few minutes later, he rode up to Moses Jackson. He lay face up with eyes wide open, a huge splotch of blood soaking the left side of his shirt and vest under his open coat. The man was dead.

For a moment, Jay studied the older man, remembering their encounter years before. In death, the man looked oddly peaceful. His face lacked the sharp-edged features Jay remembered. Ten years ago, the man was slender and hard with a narrow face. Now his face was full and round, his hair was gray and thin, and his body looked maybe twenty or thirty pounds heavier. No doubt, the past ten years had softened all of Gallagher's men, but he knew their killer instinct had not been dulled. No matter what Jackson looked like in death, his posse was a group of cold-blooded killers willing to sacrifice defenseless women and children to get him.

A simmering hatred gripped Jay for a moment, and he glared down at the dead man. He planned to see all of Gallagher's men dead, just like this man. He'd brook no discussion with any of them and take no prisoners.

It bothered Jay the marshal had only sent one man. That just didn't make any kind of sense at all. Perhaps he had sent others back the other way. Or perhaps others were trailing Jackson. Maybe Jackson was just a scout, a careless one at that, and the others were waiting up ahead for him to report back.

Jay knew of Gallagher's reputation. He was the very definition of crafty, and Jay would have to use every trick he knew to confuse them and then invent some new tactics along the way to survive. As he gazed down at Jackson's body, he knew instantly how he could gain the advantage.

He climbed carefully from his saddle and knelt beside the man. There was a serenity to the man in death. Up close, Jason had difficulty hating the man. Black lawmen were so rare on the frontier, he regretted being the cause of this man's demise. On the other hand, the deputy followed his marshal of his own free will. He didn't have to come hunting Jay after all these years.

Jay pulled the man's badge from his coat. He wondered what had put the men on his trail again after all that time. Maybe someone had reported seeing him. It hadn't been a coincidence the posse showed up in Rosebud. Their posture was aggressive, but a couple of the men had hesitated in drawing, including the marshal himself. Jay figured while they were looking for him, they hadn't actually expected to find him in Rosebud. It didn't matter. The posse now knew exactly where he lived.

Jay wondered if the deputy had a wife or children wherever he lived. If he was successful in dispatching the rest of the posse, their wives or children might never discover what had become of the men. It was a hell of a thing to do to a family. They had kissed their men goodbye not knowing they'd never see them again. *How long would they wait until they got on with their lives?*

That was one of the unfortunate consequences of taking up the manhunt, but there'd be no explaining it to a widow and her children. Maybe they'd eventually hear it was Jason Peares who killed their men. Maybe the kids would grow up harboring hatred and would begin their own manhunt. Jay shook off those thoughts.

After wiping the blood from Jackson's long coat, he tried it on for size along with the man's hat. Moses Jackson was a big man, and his hat was much too big for Jay, but at some distance Gallagher's men wouldn't notice the coat draped on him like a blanket. By the time he was close enough for them to recognize him, it would be too late for some of them. They'd know their comrade was dead, and the emotion of that knowledge would make them hesitate. Maybe their fury would cause them to make another mistake. Maybe his deception would already have claimed another one or two of the posse.

Jay mounted up again and sweet-talked his way to Jackson's horse. As he inventoried the pack, he whistled. He found three knives, two rifles, two Colt forty-fives, and a box of a hundred rounds *for each weapon*. There was enough dried beef and hardtack to last almost a month in the deputy's bulging saddle bags. Four canteens, one change of clothes, a bedroll, and a rain slicker finished out the man's kit.

He knew these were serious hunters, and now he realized they had spared no expense to find and kill him. He had no doubt the other members of the posse were similarly equipped. If so, each man outgunned him two to one. If they caught him in an extended shootout or holed him up somewhere, they could outlast him on food and ammunition alone. He decided to take Jackson's supplies with him. The extra mount would slow him down or even hinder him if he needed to move in a hurry but having a fresh mount to switch up along with the supplies would be worth the risk.

Jay started moving again but kept off the main trail. He was always wary of possible ambushes, but after another day and a half of riding, he encountered no one else. It just didn't fit.

*Where are the others? Could they possibly be so inept as to send a single rider after me? Have the years dulled their common sense?* He couldn't imagine Gallagher doing something so reckless. *I must be missing something, some critical strategy I just can't see.*

Turning his attention to the manhunt, Jay tried to deduce where the men would camp the coming night. He found their camp from the previous night in a narrow, dead-end canyon. Jay expected as much since the canyon had only one entrance and was easily defended. Its steep walls would be hard for an intruder to navigate without noise.

The next day, their trail continued southeasterly until it joined up with another road leading north to a town Jay had never visited over the neighboring mountain ridge to the east. It was the ideal route for Gallagher, since a trail through the mountains would put Jay in danger of any number of ambushes. He would have to travel slowly and very carefully.

Then Gallagher and his men did the impossible. To Jay's complete surprise, they turned south! His surprise deepened further when he studied their tracks. He discerned distinct tracks for six separate riders. All the men were riding together. No one was watching the back trail or waiting in ambush for him. They'd ridden into Rosebud nine strong, but he'd killed Bo Madison and one other, and later dispatched Moses Jackson. Only six remained.

Before mounting up again, Jay let his gaze sweep the trail behind him. Maybe Gallagher hadn't ridden into Rosebud with all his men after all. It would be like him to leave some men outside in reserve and now to have those extra men hanging back.

Regardless, the posse took the well-traveled road straight toward the New Mexico border and picked up their pace, moving fast across nearly wide-open flat land. This told Jay they knew the lay of the land and where they were going, but it seemed just the opposite of what they *should* be doing.

If they suspected Jay was following, they should have tried to gain ground fast during the first couple of days while Jay would be forced to ride slower to avoid possible traps. With the next few days on familiar territory, common sense would have them ride slower and rest frequently to conserve their horses' stamina.

Jay began to get an unsettling feeling. Somehow, Gallagher was working some kind of trick strategy on him, except he couldn't figure it out. If he wasn't going up against an ultimate professional, he would have laughed at such an amateurish tactic. But he knew the moment he got careless, he would end up dead.

Gallagher's tactic hit him like a bullet. Moses Jackson had to have been a decoy. He was bait. Fortunately for Jay, neither the marshal nor Jackson knew he had a long rifle. No doubt, Jackson figured he'd have plenty of warning to avoid getting shot.

Jay's conclusions fit well with his previous thoughts. Gallagher left his extra men behind him, and he was trying to lure him into a state of overconfidence by feigning poor strategy. Jay smiled to himself and decided to give them just what they wanted, but in a way they would never expect. He decided to do the unthinkable, the totally reckless. He would ride through the night and outrun whoever was following him. He would then catch Gallagher and his men at their next camp at sunrise.

Jay knew this territory also. As the hills sank into the flatland, there would be no more defensible canyons. He was betting Gallagher would settle his men in the flatland on the far side of the hills. The wide-open land would be easily defended since no one could ride up without being heard by the lookouts sure to be posted during the night.

When dawn came, Jay would have a surprise for Gallagher. Even as his strategy tumbled through his brain, Jay recalled something else from the chase ten years ago. He had only fragmented memories about the posse and the chase, primarily because most of the time he was simply running for his life. But there was one encounter that left a clear impression on him about the skinny man. Slim Jim was his name. Jay saw him briefly in Rosebud, and the man still had his red hair and beard, though both were thinned out considerably with age.

Jay smiled with confidence in his new plan and spurred his horse faster.

# CHAPTER 8

GALLAGHER STRETCHED BOTH ARMS OVER his head in a mighty yawn, then sucked in the crisp, cool air. He eyed his men as they prepared morning coffee. This morning there was extra cursing and disagreeable comments. Billy Hutchinson had the cooking duty.

"Mornin', Marshal."

Gallagher turned as the other Hutchinson rode in from his roving patrol.

"Any trouble about?"

"Not a bit," Robert Hutchinson replied, dismounting. "No sign of anything out of the ordinary." He swept his arm around the plains. Only two hills were within sight. The nearest was almost two-thirds of a mile away and the other rose above and behind the first. They had clear sight and nearly an uninterrupted field of fire for almost a mile in all directions.

Robert turned away, adding, "Hell, who would even try?" The man led his horse to where the others were picketed. "Who's cooking this morning? I'm starvin'."

Somebody hollered, "Your brother!"

"Sheee-it! Just shoot me now and put me out of my misery."

A chorus of laughter erupted from the campfire and Billy threw his hat at his brother.

Gallagher bundled his coat flaps tighter around him and worked his numb fingers inside his gloves as he surveyed the surrounding land.

"Cold this morning, eh, Marshal?"

Willie Smith stole his attention momentarily. He, too, was bundled inside his long coat. Their breath frosted in the cold air.

"A bit."

"Not like when we were young. We could camp out like this all year long and never think nothing of it."

Gallagher nodded solemnly. "Use to be this was undershirt weather."

Smith reached a gloved fist around to work the kinks out of the small of his back. "Hell, twenty years ago, I could sleep on a flat rock without a bedroll or even a blanket. Not anymore. I'm aching all over."

"Yeah, I know what you mean. My shoulders are a might stiff too."

"I reckon we're getting too old for this."

"Yeah."

Gallagher turned his attention back to the landscape. He thought again about his pending retirement. Then his wife's lovely face filled his inner vision. She had finally coaxed him into hanging up his guns and his badge. She had planned a nice retirement party at the courthouse for the end of the month. The whole town was invited, and she'd even received some notes from all over the county from folks who wanted to attend.

Gallagher smiled inwardly as he caught a whiff of brewing coffee. She'd worked on him for a couple of years, but the truth was easy for him to accept. Retirement was a comfortable decision to arrive at. He was getting old. He could feel it in his bones. Even more, he felt he'd completed his life's work. The town and the county were safe and had been for years. He hadn't been on a manhunt for nearly three years.

His gaze hardened as he thought about why he was again riding the trail on a manhunt at the ripe age of fifty-eight. He considered the criminal named Charles Strange. He clenched his gloved fists and started to feel the squeeze in his chest again as he fondly remembered Lizzy. She was the only woman he'd ever loved. She was the only woman he'd ever kissed. Then he thought about his son.

Gallagher closed his eyes for a moment. The land was not nearly as lawless nowadays as it had been just ten years back. The westward spread of civilization, with its laws and rules of behavior, had pretty much tamed the frontier. Gallagher had chosen law enforcement as his career when he was barely a man. Over the decades, he had contributed significantly to the taming of the frontier, but his was a violent career putting him in the crosshairs of danger more times in one year than most folks faced in their entire lives. He never imagined he'd outlive his own son, a young man who had chosen the same violent career.

Now he'd outlived his wife. Another casualty of his life's work. He didn't know how he was going to live without her, or if he even wanted to. He pounded his right fist into his left palm in frustration. That's when he thought he saw a flash at the far left edge of his sight, like sunlight reflecting off metal. His brain told him a reflection was impossible, as the sun had yet to break the eastern horizon. His ears registered a passing zip and a thump, but his attention was distracted by a sudden commotion at the campfire.

Robert Hutchinson seemed to have tripped over something and stumbled forward, arms flailing. He caught hold of Steve Pickens, almost hugging the shorter man. His mouth slobbered over the top of Pickens's forehead before Pickens reacted by shoving Hutchinson off him.

"Get off me, you crazy fool!"

Pickens pushed Hutchinson away and the man stumbled backward out of control, arms flailing and legs wobbling. Even as Gallagher watched the man begin to fall over backward, he heard another zip followed by another thump and Hutchinson jerked straight again as if slammed in the back by a giant, invisible fist. Blood and gore exploded from the front of Hutchinson's coat. Gallagher and his men froze, then a deep boom thundered in from the distance, followed closely by another as Hutchinson finally crumbled to his knees and fell face down.

Gallagher turned toward the sound in the distance and saw another flash. Instinctively, he knew the next shot was meant for him. He spun to the ground as another bullet zipped through the air he had just occupied. Steve Pickens grunted loudly and stumbled back a few steps before falling to the ground clutching his chest.

"Take cover!" Gallagher shouted the warning over the booming sound of the third shot. His men grabbed rifles and guns and dove behind the few bushes or rocks they could find, most pitifully too small to provide any protection.

"He's gotta be half a mile away!" Billy Hutchinson said.

"Farther," Slim Jim said as he ran to the neatly stacked saddle packs near the horses and pulled out his Sharps long rifle from its scabbard. On the run to the nearest tree, he snapped up the front and rear sights and worked in a single shell and slammed the bolt home. After a few seconds of adjustment to his sights, he was ready.

"Where is he?" Slim Jim demanded.

Gallagher pulled out the spyglass he always carried in his coat and extended it to its full length. He settled down beside Slim Jim. Both men lay prone with barely half of their bodies protected by the thick tree trunk. Gallagher peeked to the right of the trunk and Slim Jim aimed from the left. The marshal focused his telescoping spyglass into the distance as Slim Jim quickly peeled his glove from his right hand.

"He's on top of that near hill, about a hand's width to the right of that big boulder...*your* right, not *his* right. Can you get him from here?"

"Hell, yes. It's a long shot, but I can get him." He paused. "There he is." He worked his rear sight again. "He's all mine."

Over the decades, Gallagher had learned to keep his left eye open while he examined distant sights through the spyglass with his right eye. That way his peripheral vision could still see what was happening around him. Gallagher was aware Slim Jim took a deep breath and slowly let out half as he applied even pressure to the trigger. His left eye registered the man squint through his rifle sights even as his right eye against the spyglass saw another flash from Jason Peares's distant rifle. Gallagher barely had time to flinch when the tree trunk in front of him exploded just as Slim Jim's rifle barked. He gasped in horror at Slim Jim's convulsing body.

In all his years, he'd never seen such a thing. He stared in disbelief at the ragged fist-sized hole in the thick tree trunk. Bark and splinters puckered outward from the hole. The bullet had punched *clean through the tree!*

Ignoring the danger from the distant long rifle, he raised up and turned his friend's still body over. The bullet had entered Slim Jim's prone body just above the right shoulder, between the side of his head and the rifle stock, then had ripped down through the inside of his chest and belly.

Gallagher knew quite a bit about the ballistics of bullets. Long rifles, especially, often used heavier bullets, and they were usually propelled by a stronger load of powder. The amount of energy carried by a long rifle shot was tremendous, and the man's insides had probably been scrambled up like boiled grits. Death for his friend had been mercifully quick.

Still, he had never fully appreciated the penetrating power of a sniper rifle until just that moment. Jason Peares had to be using .50-caliber shells, maybe even .54 or .58, like army snipers used. Slim Jim always used .44 caliber shells, and his Sharps rifle had a standard thirty-six-inch barrel, more than adequate for most law enforcement tasks. If Jason Peares was using a military-grade Sharps or Spencer with a forty-inch or longer barrel, Gallagher and his men were far outclassed.

Anger boiled up in Gallagher as he looked up to where he knew Jason Peares was perched. He saw another flash and dove aside as another chunk of the tree he was hiding futilely behind exploded in his face. Gallagher grabbed his friend's sniper rifle and ran for his horse.

"Withdraw! Everybody move! Zig zag!"

"What about our packs!"

"Leave 'em! He'll pick us off with ease if we even try!"

Shot after shot rained in from the distant hill. The posse ran for their horses as silent bullets zipped by every three or four seconds. The distant threat was made all the more eerie by the delayed thunder from the gunfighter's rifle.

Gallagher saw Willie Smith scrambled over to Pickens's still thrashing body and start to carry him over to a horse. Before he even got two steps with his heavy load, another bullet slammed into the wounded man. Smith finally dropped the man, and Gallagher knew Pickens was dead or soon would be. The marshal mounted his horse and leaned down sideways to grab a saddle pack on the run. He couldn't keep it in his grip, though, so he raced away to follow the others.

He brought up the rear as his posse rounded a low rise in the otherwise flat ground, just over a mile from the camp. He stopped and gazed back toward the camp. He withdrew a spyglass from his pack and put the brass fixture to his eye. A tiny figure stood in clear view atop the distant hill. It looked like the man was wearing Moses Jackson's gray long coat.

Through his spyglass he watched as Jason Peares rode down into camp, discarded Jackson's overcoat, and sat before the campfire. He seemed heedless of the dead bodies and casually helped himself to their uneaten breakfast and coffee, periodically staring into the distance at Gallagher. The man even had the gall to raise his coffee cup toward him in a toast.

*Bastard!*

Gallagher realized all the hatred he had suppressed over the years for this murdering outlaw killer still simmered within him. Now it came boiling to the surface and he knew before he attended to the Strange Scalpers, he would kill Jason Peares.

# CHAPTER 9

"**D**ARN FOOLS CAN'T COOK WORTH a damn," Jay muttered to himself. "That's for sure."

The marshal hadn't been so smart after all. Jay considered his situation as he began to eat the posse's food. In fact, the man's strategy had been downright ignorant. There were no traps, no ambushes. First, he'd sent a lone deputy, Moses Jackson, back to kill him. Then he simply left a clear path for Jay to follow and an invitation for him to kill them all. It made no sense at all. How could Gallagher possibly have thought one man could dispatch him? Maybe the marshal was going senile. Maybe Moses Jackson was too. Hell, maybe they all had forgotten about Jay's gunfighter reputation. Maybe ten years had dulled their respect for his skills.

In the end, it didn't matter to Jay. Even though he had missed the marshal three times, he had to admit he liked his new odds. He felt confident now facing only three hunters. *Those are survivable odds,* he thought, as he stuffed another spoonful of overcooked potatoes and beef in his mouth. He gagged and almost spit the nasty food out but thought better of it. A man riding the trail never knew when he would be able to get another meal.

Jay stared at Gallagher in the distance and raised his cup in a mock toast. He washed down the food with a big swallow of the hot, strong coffee. The marshal and his two survivors had had their last meal for a couple days. It would take them that long to reach the next town down the road. Jay considered the impossible. He'd learned a lot about the man and his methods when the marshal pursued him ten years back. It wasn't unreasonable to expect him to be bold and try to retake his supplies.

After Gallagher finally rode off to join the rest of his fleeing posse, Jay looked around the camp and scavenged through all the packs. He had three more of the posse's horses and all their packs. Gallagher and his two remaining men were at a serious disadvantage. Between the three of them, they had only a handful of guns, but no food or water. They'd have to endure the long ride bareback through mountain trails and switchbacks, a tough challenge even for young men. The old posse would be fairly uncomfortable in less than a week.

This last revelation was more than Jay could possibly hope for. Though they were organized and as efficient as an army detachment, he was guessing between the three of them, they probably didn't have enough money to buy food, supplies, ammunition, or even used saddles.

Jay had another helping of their food and washed it down with equally distasteful coffee. He gathered all the food, supplies, and money bags and packed one horse with as many supplies as he could fit on the animal's back. Next, he threw the rest of the saddles, packs, and weapons in a pile and set it afire.

Jay's final plan was to add despair to Gallagher's plight. They might try to retake their supplies but would only find charred debris. Jay thought to scatter the remaining two horses, but they were likely well trained and might return to camp. He could take them with him, but sooner or later they would become a burden and he would have to set them loose. He couldn't afford the luxury of humanity and risk having the animals finding their way to their owners again. Gallagher and his men would grant him no quarter, so neither would he give them any.

With regret, Jay shot the two horses. He piled the dead deputies with the animal carcasses and started another blaze. *More husbands or fathers or brothers would never return home to their loved ones,* he thought. He paused at the sight of Slim Jim. The man was an excellent sharpshooter in his own right. He recalled his narrow escape years ago as Slim Jim sent bullets after him from his Sharps sniper rifle. The memory led him to eliminate the sharpshooter early in his assault on their camp. He had no doubt Gallagher realized the enormity of Jay's victory. He nodded at the corpse, giving the professional a measure of respect.

In the distance, he knew Gallagher and his men would see the smoke and would know exactly what it meant. There was no treasure waiting to be reclaimed. Hopelessness would be a powerful weapon for Jay and an equally powerful demoralizer for Gallagher's men. He had added that significant mental victory to his two overwhelming encounters with the hunters.

Jay wondered again about Gallagher's erratic tactics. *Why would his posse follow a deranged old man who had taken leave of his senses? Loyalty was one thing, but stupidity was another issue altogether. The whole posse couldn't be insane or driven by hatred, could they?*

The smart thing for Gallagher to do was to continue south and attempt to resupply as soon as possible, then take up pursuit of Jay again. The man hadn't been very smart so far though. He was a man driven by blind hatred, and he'd shot up a town of innocents to get his target. Then he'd led his men into a hapless ambush, so Jay figured he wasn't any more likely to choose the smart option the next time.

The more Jay considered his tactical situation, the more certain he was Gallagher was obsessed. He was hungry for revenge, so he would not run. Altogether, Jay had killed six of his posse. The marshal would be angry. He would go on the offensive.

Jay thought back over the years, of all the hunts Gallagher was reputed to have conducted. Except for one target, he always got his man. Jay was the singular exception. From personal experience, he knew Gallagher would not give up. Jay had been lucky in the mountains of northern California those many years ago, or Gallagher would have gotten him as well.

Jay suddenly decided to change his plan. He redistributed most of the supplies between his horse and Jackson's mount. He added the rest of his scavenged supplies to the fire and shot the extra horse. He mounted up and reversed his previous course to head north, away from Gallagher, then traveled west toward snowcapped peaks in the distance.

He knew Gallagher would follow him, whether or not the lawman had supplies. He would live off the land if necessary to catch his man. Jay had inadvertently chased them out of Rosebud, temporarily putting them on the defensive, and for whatever reason, caught them unawares at their camp. Though they had committed a costly tactical blunder, Jay knew they wouldn't repeat it.

Now, at least for the moment, Jay was on the defensive. That was part of his plan. He would remain on the defensive only until the time was right to strike. Then he would lure Gallagher's posse into another trap. The irony was not lost on Jay.

He was a hunted man again.

Gallagher called his men to a halt after an hour of hard riding south. He was fuming inside, and he was sure his men could see his anger. Jason Peares had caught them with their pants down. The man saw through his plan and killed Moses Jackson probably without even exchanging any words. He then second-guessed their camp.

Gallagher was angry more at himself than at his adversary. It was the most logical defensible camp strategy for someone familiar with the territory. Now he knew Jason Peares was also familiar with the territory. It was a costly error. He had lost some of his best friends, but the lessons learned were valuable.

"Jason Peares isn't taking prisoners, and he isn't looking for any conversation."

"Then we shouldn't either," added Willie Smith. "Shoot to kill."

Gallagher nodded and looked over at the sullen Billy Hutchinson. "How 'bout you?"

"You know where I stand." Hutchinson looked from one man to the other. "He killed my brother. He's got to pay. I was wondering how long we were going to run away."

"Just long enough to make him think he's got us beat."

"He likely won't fall for that, Marshal," Hutchinson said. "He knows you too well."

"What about the Strange Scalpers?" Smith asked.

"If we don't find Jason Peares, he'll continue to hunt us at his leisure, and we'll never get the opportunity to finish our business with the Scalpers. We take care of him first, then we go after Charles Strange." The men nodded.

"He's burning up all our supplies," Hutchinson said, pointing back along the trail.

Gallagher and Smith turned and saw the black smoke in the distance.

"He's trying to discourage us, send us down south to resupply so he can ambush us again." Gallagher shook his head. "But we know something he doesn't know. We've got enough to survive on for a while."

"Right," Smith said. He spread his coat apart and found a handful of beef jerky sticks and gum in his inner pockets. Hutchinson jiggled his outer pockets and was rewarded by the sound of metal clinking together.

"I've got fifty shots and enough grub for three days."

"Good. Then all we need is water."

"We'll have to stay close to the streams until we can kill some varmint. We can use the skins or intestines for water bags."

Gallagher nodded. "He'll know that, so we better be careful. He'll figure we'll turn back and strike his trail, so he'll head north and maybe east or west, try to get behind us."

"Then let's move like we got a purpose, Marshal."

"I'll take the point first. If we get him up in the winding mountain trails, we can neutralize his long rifle. Any questions?" Gallagher looked around, but neither of the men spoke. "Then let's go get him."

Five days and nights passed. Jay rode slowly, changing mounts frequently to keep his horses fresh. Now he was glad he had left the third pack horse behind. Fully laden, it would have tired quickly on the steep trails and would have slowed Jay too much. He wanted to ride slow enough so Gallagher could stay within reach, but not so slow the posse would gain ground.

*They'll be very uncomfortable by now,* Jay thought with satisfaction.

Their bellies would be growling from hunger. If they were gathering edible plants as they rode, they'd have to be plenty tired of berries or tree leaves by now. Jay knew some varieties of plant food, though nutritious, could cause stomach cramps or other discomforts. Jay knew from personal experience stomach cramps could weaken even the strongest of men. It would make them prone to mistakes. Despite any discomfort, the posse would eat whatever food they could find, not knowing when or if they'd find game to kill.

Without saddles to insulate the men from the horses' rump movement, they would be nursing sore butts and chaffed inner thighs by now. As the animals labored uphill, sweat would be soaking through the men's pants, resulting in blisters. Lack of stirrups would only compound that problem as well as give their aging leg muscles extended exercise as they clung to their animals.

*Yes, the old men should be mighty uncomfortable right about now.*

Every now and again, Jay paused to make sure the posse took the correct fork whenever the trail split. Though he was sure Gallagher was an expert tracker, he didn't want to lose them or make following him too difficult. He wanted to keep them motivated. He could see them far below him in the distance, a couple miles back. Tiny specks moving against the rocks and bushes.

He was sure they could see him clearly also, as he frequently crested hills against a backdrop of the higher snowcapped peaks.

His plan was simple, and he knew Gallagher would acknowledge its simplicity as well. Years ago, he narrowly escaped the posse by making a last desperate dash into a snowswept valley. The drifts were too deep for the posse's horses to traverse, but they were just hardpacked enough for him to sled across.

He wanted Gallagher to think he was hoping for another escape through the high mountain snow. This time, Jay had other plans to lead Gallagher into an unsuspecting trap. He would kill the last of the posse and return to Rosebud. Then he'd hang up his guns for good.

Gallagher called a halt as they came to the trail marker proclaiming Rocky Forest Town – 3 Miles. It pointed down a side trail to the south. The ground was muddy from snowmelt and a single set of tracks led straight ahead as the trail they were on continued to the west.

Hutchinson dismounted and studied the tracks. "He's still a couple of hours ahead of us. I don't like this, Marshal. With an extra mount to switch up, he could have been long gone by now. Hell, he *should* have been long gone."

Gallagher nodded. "I think he's trying to lure us up high without supplies." He paused for a moment, thinking. "These trails aren't as winding as I thought they might be. If Jason Peares gets a long stretch of trail up ahead, we'll be hard-pressed to keep after him for an extended pursuit with no supplies."

Gallagher paused as he considered the sniper rifle tied to the flank of Willie Smith's horse. Neither he nor his men were half as accurate as Slim Jim had been.

Smith nodded. "That may have been his plan all along."

Gallagher stroked his beard. "I think he's teasing us. He wants to keep us after him, keep moving higher into the cold and snow."

"Well, he's giving us a choice, Marshal," Smith said. "We'll lose at least three more hours if we take this trail down to town and resupply."

Gallagher nodded. "He knows that too. With a five hour lead on us, he can disappear anywhere in these mountains. It could take us weeks to track him down. Or he'll be able to backtrack and ambush us." He glanced up the trail to the west, then down the southern trail. "But we need supplies badly."

"Yeah," Hutchinson added. "That's why he burned ours up."

"We'll split up," Gallagher said. "You two take what little money we have and get some food and water."

Willie Smith jingled the coins in his pant pocket. "Won't buy much."

"More than we have now," Hutchinson said.

"I'll continue up the trail to make sure he doesn't double back on us. Any trouble either up here or down your way, fire a single warning shot. The echo will carry for miles up here in these canyons. Then we'll regroup right here. Questions?"

A few silent seconds passed, and all three men unceremoniously kicked their horses into motion. Gallagher followed the clear tracks up the trail, higher into the mountains, for the next hour. Suddenly, an icy panic gripped his gut as the tracks of Jason Peares's horse veered off the main trail and followed a narrow path downhill. Then he saw the second sign tacked to a tree.

Rocky Forest Town – 2 miles

He had underestimated the outlaw killer yet again. Jason Peares knew of the shortcut and would be in town waiting when his men arrived. Gallagher raised his rifle and squeezed the trigger, but nothing happened. The firing pin had jammed. He tried to reload and free the mechanism, but it would not fire. He tossed the useless weapon aside in rage and spurred his horse down the steep path. Recklessly, he tore down into the valley, ignoring the steep and narrow path and treacherous turns. He was briefly aware of the near vertical drop to his right, but he pressed on, riding fast. His men needed him.

# CHAPTER 10

**A**FTER STASHING HIS HORSES NEAR the trail on the far west end of town, Jay walked quickly and cautiously up the narrow dirt path functioning as the town's main road. He adjusted his double-gun holster as he walked past the empty barn. He saw only one horse on the road. It was tied in front of the saloon.

Gallagher and his men had not arrived yet, but they couldn't be far away unless they hadn't taken the bait. Jay was betting Gallagher and his men needed supplies more than revenge at the moment and would be along in short order. He discovered the general store was next door to the saloon where he would wait. They would ride straight past, he was sure, because if they had any money at all, they would spend it on supplies rather than on drink.

Jay stopped suddenly in front of the dust-covered window of the saloon and smiled. What he saw there convinced him perhaps they would have a drink anyway. He opened the door and went in, quickly scanning the small room as he walked straight to the bar. A huge bear of a man sat at one of the two tables with his back to the door. His head rested across his folded arms and his hat shaded the side of his face.

The barkeep was a frail-looking, older man who wore round wire-rimmed glasses making him look more like a banker than a bartender. He sat on a bar stool in front of the bar. A few unkempt strands of hair were all that remained atop his head. As

Jay walked up to him, the barkeep raised a single finger to his lips and nodded to the sleeping man.

Jay nodded and whispered. "Have you got anything to write with? Maybe some wood and some coal chunks." Jay eyed the stove in the center of the wall opposite the bar as he dropped several coins on the countertop. "I want to make a sign for my friends who'll be arriving soon."

"How 'bout a quill and some paper?"

Jay raised his eyebrow in surprise. He hadn't expected to find writing instruments in a lazy mountain town like this one.

"Perfect."

The barkeep stepped away from his stool, walked behind the bar, and produced a small bottle of ink with an honest-to-goodness, old-fashioned, feathered writing pen. He placed the quill and a large piece of paper on the bar. Jay quickly made his sign and placed it in the window, so it stuck in the gap between the cracked glass and the window frame. Then he took a seat at the second table and waited.

Crazy Willie Smith and Billy Hutchinson rode slowly up the road toward the general store. Willie Smith reined up and pointed to the saloon window. Hutchinson smiled.

"Let me buy you a drink, my friend."

"Gladly, but only if you let me buy you one first."

The men laughed as they dismounted and left their horses ground-tied in front of the saloon. They paused in the doorway and noticed two sleeping men at the tables, hats covering their faces. They both walked over to the bar and laid their rifles on the countertop.

"Your sign says free drinks," Willie Smith said smiling.

"Today only," added Hutchinson. "And that's good because we're woefully short of money." They both chuckled.

The bartender wordlessly poured two glasses full of nearly clear whiskey.

"What's the special occasion?" Willie Smith asked.

The bartender shrugged. "Compliments of your friend."

"Excuse me?" Hutchinson asked.

Both men froze as they heard Jay stand behind them. They looked at each other and knew they had been suckered.

"Where's Marshal Gallagher?" Jay asked.

"He stopped at the outhouse at the end of town. He'll be here straight away."

"He'll be just in time to collect your dead bodies then."

Jay stared curiously at their backs. While he waited for them to make a move, he noticed the tattered ends of their coats. It looked as if the bottom halves had been ripped off at the waist.

The men looked at each other. Willie Smith shrugged and said, "Might as well drink up then. Be a shame to waste a drink."

"Especially if it's free." Hutchinson raised his glass in salute. "Been a pleasure, my friend."

Willie Smith nodded, and the two men emptied their glasses in a single gulp. Then they grabbed their rifles and spun. By the time they had settled their gazes on Jay, he had emptied both his guns into them. They bounced off the bar and fell forward, but Jay was out the back door before they hit the floor. He had no wish to be caught trying to reload his guns when Gallagher entered the saloon.

He ran along the back of the row of shacks, jumping over barrels and debris, and weaving around trees growing right up to the back of some of the buildings. He would not stay to fight a shootout with the marshal. Instead, he would ride away and leave the lawman to suffer his latest defeat. If Gallagher continued to pursue him, the anguish and humiliation of losing his entire posse would eat at his self-control and judgment. The next time they met, Jay would firmly have the advantage. He would then kill the lawman just as the lawman had promised to kill him.

As the thoughts swept through his mind, Jay thrashed toward his horses, still glancing behind him for the lawman to emerge from the back of the saloon. Even as he ran from behind the last shack, he heard the metallic sound in front of him. In half a heartbeat, he realized it was he who had been outsmarted.

Marshal Gallagher reached the floor of the narrow valley and rounded an outcrop of rock revealing the first of several of the small town's shacks. He saw the clearing set back in the trees, just off the path functioning as the town's main road. In the clearing, not fifty paces from the back of the nearest shack, Gallagher recognized Moses Jackson's horse. It waited beside another.

The marshal jumped from his mount even as gunshots thundered through the valley and echoed back several times off the near mountain walls. Seconds later, he heard a door slam open behind the near row of shacks, and he knew his adversary was coming back to the clearing for his horses.

He quickly swept a rifle from the scabbard of the nearest mount and smoothly worked its loader as if he were born to do that all his life. He aimed at the approaching footsteps and had the weapon set point-blank in the center of the gunfighter's chest as he ran from behind the log building.

Finally, Jason Peares had made his fatal mistake.

Gallagher pulled the trigger.

He missed.

# CHAPTER II

**A**S JAY MOVED INTO THE clearing beyond the end of the last shack, he sensed something was not as it should be. Maybe it was a gut feeling or some perception of movement where none should be. Maybe it was the faint hint of a metallic sound. Maybe he instinctively knew, on a subconscious level, the sound he heard was a weapon being readied.

He acted quickly and decisively, even before he was fully beyond the wall of the shack. Before he clearly saw Gallagher pointing his rifle at him, he ducked and spun as the bullet tugged at his coat collar. He started to spin again, but instead tripped over a tree root and slammed headfirst into another tree. As he bounced off, bark exploded exactly where his head hit the tree. Totally out of control, he tried to continue his momentum back toward the log shack wall. He drew a gun he hadn't reloaded, hoping to scare Gallagher into taking cover, but his tactic failed.

More gunfire chased him as he dove and rolled, until he was finally behind the wall again and running back toward the saloon. He tried to load a couple of shells into his gun, but he fumbled them as he scrambled to safety. Giving up, he simply holstered his gun and rushed through the saloon. With a side glance, he noticed the big man was still asleep at his table. The gunfire inside and out hadn't bothered him. Gallagher's last deputies still lay on the floor where they fell, their blood staining the age-old wood planks. The proprietor ducked behind the bar as Jay raced past him and out the front door. He leaped onto the nearest horse, grabbed the reins of the other, and raced out of town.

The horses with their makeshift saddles and stirrups reminded Jay with sickening clarity that Marshal Gallagher wasn't as helpless and uncomfortable as he had imagined. He realized as he guided the animals to the edge of town it was he, Jay, who had seriously underestimated the cleverness and resourcefulness of his opponents.

Just before he rounded the last shack to safety, he heard the shot and felt the bullet burn across his thigh and thump into the horse's flank just behind his front leg. The animal folded under Jay and went down instantly. In a panic, Jay took the impact on his shoulder and rolled, trying to jump to the side at the same time. The horse tumbled also and even through the thick sheepskin coat, he felt the horse's hoof slam him in the back like a sledgehammer.

Jay gasped as the kick knocked his breath out of him, and he careened against a tree trunk, its bark slashing the right side of his face. He bounced off the tree and managed to stay on his feet, but he saw the other horse running away from him. He tried to breathe but couldn't. With each step, he could feel his strength draining away. If he lost that horse, he was dead.

The horse veered around the boulder and angled back toward the trail. In desperation, Jay spent his last bit of breathless strength and leaped up onto a boulder just off the trail. He launched himself into the air as the animal passed the far side of the boulder. But he missed.

Even as he fell to the side, Jay grasped the animal's mane in his hands and clung for his life as the animal protested loudly and dragged him. Its front knees kicked him in the chest twice as it ran. Somehow, as darkness ringed the edges of his eyesight, Jay found his feet under him and jumped up, clawing his way onto the animal's back. He kicked the sides of the horse and held on as the animal ran swiftly back onto the main trail and headed south, away from the mountain town.

When he was finally able to breathe again, he mentally inventoried his body for new injuries. His back ached, but he doubted if the injury was anything more serious than a bruise. On the other hand, the pain in his chest, where the horse had kicked him, was sharp and piercing every time he took a deep breath. If he had cracked or broken ribs, he knew he might not live long enough to kill Gallagher or even escape him. Riding would aggravate the injury, magnifying the pain until he would be forced to stop. He would be in no shape to put up any kind of fight. Until then, he just had to ride until he could ride no more.

He could tell the bullet wound to his right thigh was just a graze. It was a minor inconvenience, but it hurt like hell. It was almost in the exact same spot where one of Gallagher's posse had grazed him in Rosebud. The side of his face was scratched and swollen from the impact with the tree, but otherwise not serious. Still, the wounds needed tending. Unfortunately, the medicine and rags Mrs. Travers gave him were in his pack on one of the horses Gallagher now claimed.

With that thought, his week-old shoulder wound reminded him of its presence with a throbbing ache. He'd been washing the wound and using the medicine as Mrs. Travers instructed, but now he would have to make do with whatever natural remedies he could find.

For many years, Jay had survived the worst man and nature could throw at him. He had learned his lessons well while living among the Arapaho Indians for several months. Hunting and being hunted, living off the land, treating injuries, and surviving the way the native people survived were all skills he had learned exceptionally well. His battle with Gallagher was no different. He would heal his wounds and continue to survive now. Knowing that didn't make the pain any less intense.

The ultimate injury was to his pride. He had sorely underestimated Marshal Gallagher. Somehow the man must have figured out his strategy. It never occurred to Jay the marshal might have known the same back road trails and followed him.

Jay should have anticipated that outcome. The marshal was extremely crafty, but Jay had ignored his own instincts and considered himself smarter than his hunters. He'd even patted himself on the back for his ingenuity and for the brilliance of his plans.

In the end, the lawman had proved his reputation was more than mere words. It was deserved. Gallagher was the ultimate hunter, just like everyone said. Jay had simply been lucky ten years ago. This time, he would need more than luck because the lawman would not quit. Gallagher was too close now. The only good news for Jay was he'd evened the odds by disposing of the rest of the posse.

Jay had thought he held the advantage for the last week, but Gallagher and his men had adapted. They were survivors also. Jay eyed the animal skin water bag draped around the horse's neck. In addition, the men had cut off half of their long coats and used strips of cloth as reins. They rolled branches and lots of leaves inside the rest of the coat fabric and fashioned makeshift saddles for the long ride. Their coat belts served as stirrups.

When he saw the two lawmen in the saloon, they were a comical sight with their tattered half coats. Now, he understood their ingenious use of all they had available. The first horse Gallagher had shot had been carrying a makeshift saddle, but the second horse Jay now rode had reins but no saddle. He must have kicked it off in his scramble to mount the horse.

Now it was Jay who rode bareback and would drink tepid water from the animal skin. It was Jay who would eat leaves and berries and whatever else he could hunt. He'd have to sleep on the hard, frozen ground without a blanket or even a saddle pack for a pillow. Hell, he no longer even had a hat to keep his head warm or dry. He had no supplies and the only shells he had to reload his guns were the few stuck in his holster belt slots.

Gallagher, on the other hand, now rode with three horses, two of which were fairly fresh since Jason had switched out the animals frequently on his ride up the steep mountain trails. The marshal would now sleep in a warm bedroll, eat salted beef or potatoes for breakfast, lunch, and dinner, have plenty of water to drink whenever he wanted, and could enjoy hot, strong coffee.

*Just as it should be,* Jay thought. Such was the price for his own stupidity. The advantage often swung quickly in the game of the hunt.

He pushed his horse at a strong pace late into the night. With fresh horses to switch up every two or three hours, Gallagher would be able to match his pace during the day, so Jay knew he had to put as much distance between them at night as he could. The lawman could be as little as an hour behind him.

The nearest town was still over a week's ride away, a border town just inside New Mexico. If he could keep his horse alive until he got there, he would make his stand in town, but that could happen only if Gallagher didn't catch up to him first. Now he understood Gallagher's commitment and what the man would endure to kill Jay. He knew also, he would have to be equally ruthless when he next met Marshal Gallagher.

Jay forced himself not to think of the lawman as a father whose son he had killed years ago. Instead, he envisioned the marshal as an obsessed man who directly blamed Jay for the misdeed. He still carried a vendetta after ten years. He had no moral difficulties at all about shooting down women and children in an attempt to satisfy his need for revenge. He hid behind a lawman's badge and had obviously convinced himself that his actions were justified no matter what the cost.

With a slow and comfortable pace, Gallagher rode south in pursuit of the outlaw killer. Under other circumstances, he might have enjoyed the opportunity to have extended morning meals and coffee after the hardship of the past few days. He had more than ample food supplies on the horses the gunfighter had packed, and he ate several times a day to get his strength and stamina back.

Any pleasure he might have felt was canceled by the rage and sorrow boiling under his skin. Everyone he cared about for the last thirty years had been taken from him. His wife had been murdered by Charles Strange, and his entire posse had been killed by the gunfighter, Jason Peares. He was no longer the scared kid the posse chased ten years ago. Jason Peares had proven he was as skilled a manhunter as any of the marshal's posse.

Gallagher dismounted by a small creek and let his mount drink its fill. The sky was bright blue, but the high peaks kept the valley trail in deep shadow. Birds fluttered here and there, and the water trickled softly over rocks. He listened to the gentle sounds for a while, then pushed his hat back and laid his forehead against the saddle.

For the first time, the thought of giving up and returning home entered his mind. Then he realized he really had no home to return to. His posse was more than a group of lawmen. They'd been his riding partners for decades. They'd raised each other's kids. They'd shared holidays. They'd even buried loved ones together. Now they were all gone. Every last one of them was dead, and now he had no one. For the first time in his life, he was totally alone.

He straightened his hat and gazed down the trail as if he could see the outlaw in the distance. The rage took hold again and all thoughts of sorrow or quitting vanished, replaced by the ten-year-old hatred he thought he'd buried deep. Though Jason Peares was no longer a wanted criminal, the man once was and always would be, an outlaw and a killer.

After burying his friends, Gallagher stayed the night in Rocky Forest Town, where he slept in a bed in the town's one-room hotel. He was the first paying customer at the dusty hotel in several months, so the owner treated him well. He was comfortable, but he still slept with a gun in his lap and a rifle propped against the bedpost, within reach. He was taking no more chances where Jason Peares was concerned. It would be just like the killer to circle back again and try to reclaim his lost supplies. Once again, he had underestimated the man's desire to kill. His last two friends had paid for his error in judgment with their lives.

He hadn't gotten much sleep that night. The faces of his dead friends invaded his mind every time he started to fall asleep. Finally, around midnight, he'd sat up in the bed realizing sleep would not come.

"As God is my witness," he said to the empty room. "I will make him pay for all his killing."

Three days out of Rocky Forest Town, Gallagher raised his collar against the stiff afternoon breeze. When the cold rain began to fall, he retrieved his own rain slicker from the pack horse the gunfighter had stolen from him. He was taking his time with the pursuit, but he knew what Jason Peares was feeling. He wouldn't know how far behind Gallagher really was. It was likely his paranoia would drive the man to assume the marshal was right behind the last turn in the road.

He would feel the pressure of not knowing where or when his hunter would show up. He would ride his horse until it dropped, not resting the animal or himself properly, in his rush to get to safety. Every shadow would be his enemy, every sound a threat to his life. By the time he got to what he believed was safety, he would be careless and weary, always looking over his shoulder for his hunter. He'd be sick with worry—a nervous wreck.

Gallagher had no sympathy for the murderous gunfighter. He reached into his vest pocket and withdrew a metal object. He examined the star blade for the millionth time. Three of its six, pointed tips were longer than the others. It was about four inches in diameter and extremely thin, with razor-sharp points and edges. Thrown with enough force, the object could be buried almost its entire width within its victim. Such had been the case with his son.

Gallagher never discovered the identity of the Chinese man who had thrown the blade. Witnesses described the man as old and sickly, and he always assumed the man had long since died. The man's blade had struck his son in the jaw, the pain and surprise freezing him just long enough for the outlaw to shoot him twice in the chest.

The two gunshots had killed his son. One ripped through his son's lung and the other severed his backbone. Had Joshua

Gallagher lived, he would have been paralyzed for the rest of his life. In the end, he suffered in great pain for two days after the shooting.

So he was not unhappy in the least that Jason Peares was riding hard and furious, feeling the pressure and stress of not knowing where his hunter was. When Gallagher felt the time was right, when the gunfighter was at his weakest, he would appear in front of the man, and the outlaw killer would pay for all the pain he had caused and for all the lives he had taken. Finally, Gallagher would have his revenge for the death of his son, Joshua Gallagher, and for the deaths of his closest friends, the only family he'd had left.

Jay was still two days out of Stewartsville, a mining town whose ore had been depleted nearly fifteen years before. Now, the town and surrounding ranches produced cattle and farm goods as moneymaking commodities. Jay had only visited the town once since settling in Rosebud and barely remembered the sprawling town. He was certain Stewartsville was where he was going to make his stand. Gallagher would follow his tracks to town and the hunter and hunted would finally settle their differences. Jay had easily decided how he would handle the marshal. There would be no discussion or explanation of past actions, nor would he attempt to apologize for his son's death. He wouldn't try to reason with the man.

In fact, he planned to kill the man from a distance, if he could. The marshal was too dangerous an adversary to get into a close quarters gunfight with. He was too crafty and too experienced and too lucky. In a fair fight, Jay would easily hold the advantage, but the marshal wouldn't let Jay use his skill of the fast draw.

Jay didn't know when or where Marshal Gallagher would initiate the final confrontation, though he hoped he could outlast the man and at least force the event to occur on his own terms.

The lawman might be a mile behind him, or a day or more. As he did every night for the past week, Jay rode his horse until almost midnight, but he tried not to tax the animal beyond its limits. If he were in Gallagher's position, he'd take his time in the pursuit of his prey. He'd switch out horses and patiently follow his target and, with the supplies he'd taken back from Jay, he'd eat and rest well along the way. He'd let the hunted feel the pressure of not knowing when or where his pursuer was.

Jay was reasonably sure Gallagher would use this tactic. Panic and stress could sap the strength from even the strongest of men, and Jay had used this tactic himself many times over the years during his pursuits and evasions. So while Jay rode his horse long into the night, he kept his mount at a slow pace, steadily consuming the miles. He wasn't panicked, and he rested and watered his horse as frequently as he could.

He cooked the day's catch, a jackrabbit, and ate the tasty meat slowly. He savored the gamey flavor and finally washed it down with water from a stream he crossed earlier in the day. Just before he settled down to get four hours of sleep, he practiced his calming exercises taught to him by Liu Wang. The elderly railroad worker traveled with him for a few months during Jay's early days on the run from the law.

Jay took a deep breath and resisted the temptation to worry and wonder about his pursuer. Instead, he began to plan out his next day. The horse was nearing its end. After four days of long riding, it no longer ate much at night or during the very brief rest stops during the day, and it barely drank at the stream. Jay wondered if the animal would last two more days. He had little choice but to continue pressing the horse.

While Gallagher might or might not be right behind him, he couldn't afford to take the chance and slow his progress. There was nothing he could do to make things easier for the horse. All he could do was keep his wits and stay mentally alert. He had to coax the animal to last just two more days.

Tonight, instead of clearing his mind completely as he normally did, he chose to dwell on Liu Wang. It had been a long time since he had given the old man his due. For the brief time Jay spent with the old man, he grew accustomed to hearing the man's philosophical views on life and his ever-present Chinese proverbs and words of wisdom

Jay drifted back in time before Marshal Gallagher hunted him ten years ago and even before he killed Sheriff Gallagher. He drifted back before he met Liu Wang and even before he became an outlaw. He went back to the beginning, to the fateful hunting trip thirteen years ago.

# CHAPTER 12

## THIRTEEN YEARS AGO

YOUNG JASON PEARES LED HIS horse and pack mule around to the front of the tiny log cabin. The sun was just coming up and frost decorated everything from grass to bushes. A wisp of smoke wafted up lazily from the chimney and the crisp fragrance of burning firewood reminded Jason why he loved living far away from civilization.

Snow would come soon. Whatever game he caught this trip would have to last the family for many weeks. Ma and Pa waited for him on the front porch.

After words of farewell, Jason leaned over to hug the little round woman and kissed her rosy cheek. He shook his pa's hand. He hadn't hugged the man in years, not since he was a little boy. His pa said men don't hug. They show love in other ways. Jason knew no other fathers to compare his own to, but still he felt something was missing from his relationship with his pa, though he couldn't have put it into words if he was asked.

His father checked his one-legged balance by leaning heavily on his cane. He put his arm around his wife's waist. They contrasted sharply—he was dark as the night, and she was white as snow. Jason rode away with one final glance over his shoulder. He couldn't have guessed that would be the last time he'd ever see them alive. At the time, the rare sight of both his parents smiling arm in arm and his pa looking proud had filled young Jason with emotion.

The two pack mules were tied together so that one could follow the other on a single track. He led the front animal by a rope tied to the back of his saddle pack and rode off to the Cumberland Forest and the lake to find game for food. The rolling hills were really tree-covered low mountains, and Jason knew game would be plentiful there. There were still only a few settlers this far out in the wilderness, even though Wayne City was only a day's ride to the east.

This was the land of promise, his pa had said. Education was the key. Here, Negro children could go to the same schools as White children. Get your schooling, his pa always said, and you could be more in life than just a servant.

Jason suspected the real reason his pa moved the family out into the wilderness was because nobody out there cared that his pa had married a White woman and raised half-breed children. Nobody in these parts took sides or cared what color your skin was, so long as you could do your fair share of the hard work. Sometimes Jason wondered how his father managed to do his share with only one leg, but he guessed that was what sons were for.

He believed his father about schooling, and he studied extra hard. He could read and do arithmetic and science as well as anyone. He dreamed of going to college someday so he could make a difference. He was going to do something special with his life and make his mark on history. He dreamed about being famous. He didn't know how or when, but someday he knew he would make that dream come true. Maybe he could be a doctor or a dentist or something.

By the first nightfall at the lake, Jason had killed seven squirrels, four rabbits, a possum, and two deer. Each deer was just about as big as a pack mule, but he finally managed to tie them on. He decided to camp for the night and make the return trip home before sunrise. Jason awoke shivering in his bedroll amidst heavy frost long before sunrise and was almost home when the sun finally started lighting up the sky. Nothing could have prepared him for what he found.

The forest thinned into the clearing and the house came into view first. It had been completely burned-out, except all the walls still stood. He froze and stared, not believing what he saw. He blinked hard and fast, fighting back the panic, trying to wish away the terrible sight before him.

Jason studied the signs. Whoever was responsible for this deed had set fire to the house and then shot up the place. His family had been trapped inside with no way to escape. Finally, his mother and father, his older sister, and two younger brothers had made a desperate dash to get out. They were shot down like animals. Then the men had hung his pa's body upside down, by his only leg, from the big tree in front of the cabin.

Jason found the strength to bury his family, but the event passed in a blur. He dug a single pit and as gently as he could, hauled the barely recognizable bodies in. He covered his family and for some reason he never understood, he left the grave un-marked. He didn't pray, and he didn't cry. Then he rode to town for the sheriff. It was late the next day when they returned to his home. The sheriff examined the signs as well but gave Jason the harsh reality. The Wayne City community council wasn't going to authorize a posse for any of the outlying homestead-ers. Something about not collecting enough tax money for the council support fund. He'd send out wires to neighboring towns, but that process rarely got any results. Without a description of the murderers, the sheriff said he wouldn't get any results this time either.

Jason argued with the man. He didn't care about money or support funds. He didn't care about the politics of the townsfolk, or the homesteaders, or the fact that the homesteaders viewed themselves outside of city control. But the sheriff was unrelent-ing. Most of the homesteaders barely earned enough to feed their own families and couldn't afford to contribute to the support fund, but they sometimes needed benefits from the fund. That, the lawman had said, couldn't happen. One of the benefits the homesteaders had to sacrifice, he explained, was authorization for a posse.

The killers' tracks avoided any established town and headed southwest into Tennessee and farther into Arkansas, stopping only at frontier shack towns with barely a bottle of whiskey to offer. He finally followed them up into Missouri before he lost their trail in the snow. He rode into Malden, tired and disgusted.

The town was big and had four main roads. Huge cattle pens and horse corrals and stores of all kinds dotted the landscape. Jason rode in from the south where all the houses were, then straight up the main street in search of the sheriff's office. The town was bustling with all kinds of people—the kind Jason had never seen before. Where he was from, everyone wore farmers' overalls, but here men walked around in trail clothes and riding leathers and long overcoats or dusters.

And guns.

Jason passed by a saloon. He could hear the raunchy language and music from inside and could smell the stink of tobacco and liquor. The thought of living in such a town turned his stomach. He finally found the sheriff's office six doors away from the saloon but was told he could find the lawman over in the saloon. He tied his horse to the hitching rail at the sheriff's office and walked back.

Next door to the saloon, a group of rowdy cowboy types wearing guns stopped their conversation and watched Jason approach. He walked slowly with both hands in his coat pockets, slightly stooped against the stiff winter breeze. The chill of fear washed down his spine as he noticed their concentration on him. They called him names—the kind his pa said he wouldn't have to hear if he was educated. He ignored them and just looked down at the boardwalk and walked around them. Their conversation resumed after he passed.

The rough panel doors of the saloon were tied open, and the place was packed full. The stink and smoke made Jason want to gag, but he went in anyway. He had only taken two steps inside when a heavy hand came down hard on his shoulder. He turned around to look up at a huge man in denim overalls, with long, gray hair and beard matted down around his massive belly.

"You look too young to drink, and if you ain't, your kind drinks two streets over. Now git!"

"I'm looking for the sheriff, that's all." Jason winced as the grip on his shoulder became painful.

"Maybe you didn't hear me, young feller." The man squeezed until a new voice interrupted him.

"You look a bit young to be taking on my peacekeeper."

When the man released him, Jason turned to face a tall, handsome man in a dark blue, three-piece suit. He wore a ruffled, light blue, silk shirt and black string tie. The man's dark eyes glanced up and down Jason's slender frame.

"You can leave peacefully, or this man will hurt you, understand?"

"Yes, sir," Jason answered meekly. "But I'm just looking for the sheriff is all."

The tall man looked over to the other side of the room and nodded. Jason followed his gaze to see a big man walking toward him with a badge on his vest. He became suddenly aware that the saloon was very quiet, and all eyes in the room were on him. Sweat broke out around Jason's collar and forehead as he fidgeted with his fingers. The lawman was tall and heavyset, with stocky, square shoulders and narrow eyes with prominent crow's feet. He squinted down at Jason. He looked about forty or so with blond hair that was starting to go gray. His beard and mustache were neatly trimmed.

"Well, son, you want me, you got me."

"I, uh...I was wondering if you've seen any strangers come from the east or south."

The sheriff glanced over to the saloon owner with a look of ridicule in his eyes. He looked back at Jason. A smile spread across his square face.

"We get a lot of strangers through this town. I assume you're talking about Negroes."

"They're murderers! That's what they are!" Jason spat out.

"They burned my home and killed my family. Shot 'em like animals when they tried to get out!"

"Well, I'm sorry to hear that," he glanced at the tall man in the suit again. "But how do you know they came here?"

"I lost their trail just south of here in the snow and figured they might have stopped here."

"I see," said the sheriff, feigning concern by rubbing his beard. He smiled again, revealing a perfect set of white teeth. "And who are these men?"

Jason was not prepared for the question. He stammered for an answer, any answer, but could think of nothing to say.

"Well, what do these murderers look like?"

"Well, I...." Jason hesitated.

"You do know who it was that killed your family, don't you?"

"Well, I didn't see them, Sheriff, but their tracks came here."

"And you want me to arrest everyone who rode into town today from the south or east, is that right?"

Jason was fuming now. This lawman was standing here making a fool out of him in front of everyone. They were all chuckling and snickering.

"I thought so," the sheriff concluded.

He turned to go back to his table, but Jason grabbed him by the arm.

"Wait!" he pleaded.

The big man spun back around so fast that Jason jumped back in surprise. The lawman brought up a single finger in warning.

"Now let's learn something very important here, boy. I'm sorry about your family. I really am. But listen to me close." He paused for effect and glanced around as if he were speaking to the entire room instead of only Jason. "You people just did get your freedom a couple of years back, thanks to that fool, softhearted president. So now, you all got some laws protecting you, and I hear out west they're even letting some of you buy up our land.

"Pretty soon, you're going to want to vote and get paid the

same wages as us just for doing your kind of work! Then the Chinese and the Injuns are going to start whining for equality too! Then this whole blessed, beautiful nation of ours is going straight to hell in a handbag! But if you think for one minute that I'm going to let a Negro boy come into my town and have White men arrested.... Well, you better grow up quick, boy. Now, get the hell outa here!"

Jason stood there as the sheriff turned his back and walked away. He felt the grip on his shoulder again, except this time the big man yanked him backward and propelled him through the open doors. He bounced off someone passing by and landed on his rump in the muddy street as laughter boiled from the saloon.

Jason regained his feet and tried to wipe off the mud. So this was the uncivilized frontier that his father had warned him about. The Wayne City sheriff also told him about the unsheltered reality out yonder where the laws didn't apply equally to everyone. He turned away and mounted his horse, then rode slowly back southward through Malden looking for the street leading out to the west. He made up his mind that he would never find the men who killed his family. He was better off just drifting and finding a job and a new life somewhere else.

The next couple of hours passed in a haze of confusion and sorrow. He found his way two streets over and paid for a meal. As he sat by himself, a pretty lady joined him and started flirting and asking how much money he had. She said her name was Donna and sat with him for a while. They talked a bit, and he had just told her his name and why he'd come to Malden when a bully walked in and took her from him. Said he didn't know what to do with a woman like her. Jason wallowed deeper in his misery and admitted to himself that the bully was probably right. Still, he watched as Donna left with the other man. She glanced back at him as she walked through the door.

Jason finished his meal and left. He mounted up and headed west, out of town. He took no notice of the five men watching him until one of them spoke.

"Are you cold, boy?"

"This ain't no place for kids," said another amid a chorus of jeers. His speech was slurred, and Jason could tell the man was drunk even before he saw the whiskey bottles three of the men were holding. Jason was sad and cold, so he just rode past the men and ignored them.

"Hey, come on back here. We heard you were looking for us. Since you went to all the trouble to track us all the way to Missouri, why don't you come over here and let us tell you all the fun we had with your kinfolk." The men slobbered more laughter at him.

Jason spun around in the saddle and glared at the speaker. He was short and chubby with several days' whiskers and wore only an undershirt and pants. The freezing wind didn't seem to bother him at all.

"Good target practice too," another man slobbered and gulped another swig from a bottle, spilling the liquid down his chin and onto the front of his coat. "Bang, bang!" He motioned with his index finger. "Popped 'em as they climbed out that window."

"Like horses running out of a burning barn."

Guttural laughter erupted from the men and suddenly Jason lost all control. He ripped open his snow coat and felt for the old gun in his belt but froze with fear when the loudmouth leader pulled his own gun from his holster. He tossed his whiskey bottle aside, pointed the gun at Jason, and laughed.

"Get down from that horse, boy."

Shakily, Jason did what the man said. He saw the man's thumb and trigger finger move, and he reacted fast. He reached for his own gun, not knowing why or how or what he was even doing. Shock and surprise flashed across the man's face. The first shot scared Jason. Confusion and chaos spread quickly, mixed in with shouting and cussing, then more shots followed. When he opened his eyes, four of the five killers lay dead in the street in front of him and the fifth was running up the boardwalk as fast as he could.

Jason stood there shaking, holding his smoking gun at his side. He heard footsteps behind him, felt someone grab his free arm and twist it hard behind his back and throw him to the ground. He felt the hard heel of a boot against the side of his head and a distant part of his numb brain registered the taste of mud in his mouth. Metal cuffs bound his wrists behind his back, then someone grabbed his coat collar and half-dragged him up the street. As he partially regained his feet, he stumbled past Donna and the man she had left with. He was dragged into the jail.

Wordlessly, the sheriff roughly removed the handcuffs from his hands and tossed him bodily into a small, dark cell. He slammed the barred door behind Jason before he finally spoke, his voice deep and husky.

"You'll hang in the morning, boy. You should have left it alone like I told you."

Jason lay quietly on the damp stone floor where he was thrown. The hours passed slowly in the cold, dark cell, but shortly before midnight the sound of breaking glass woke Jason from a fitful sleep. From beyond the outer door there was the sound of a brief struggle, then silence. Keys unlocked the solid door leading to the cells. A tall, dark figure moved quickly to his cell, unlocked the door, and motioned for him to move. Jason hesitated for a moment, and the hooded figure spoke.

"Your name is Jason Peares, right?"

Jason nodded.

"Sorry about your family, kid," the figure said. "You got a tough break from a bigoted sheriff who doesn't care how many people saw you shoot those men in self-defense. You can die tomorrow at sunup, or you can die in a couple of days if they catch you. The choice is yours."

The figure stepped aside and pointed toward the back door. In a stripe of moonlight coming through the front window, Jason saw it was the tall gentleman from the saloon.

"Donna works for me," he explained. He must have known the question was boiling to the surface of Jason's mind. Jason didn't even hesitate before bolting for the back door of the jail.

His horse waited for him, fully packed, and he jumped onto the animal and raced away into the darkness.

The new morning sun found him shivering in the frigid air as he rode into a new life as a fugitive from the law. The lessons of living on the run were hard, but Jason quickly learned how to survive the continuous search for food. In his travels, he also learned the name of the killer who had escaped from Malden and that the man was last known to be drifting toward Colorado. Jason didn't know what the future held for him. He only knew that his current path would take him at least as far as Colorado in search of a murderer named Scoot.

# CHAPTER 13

## TWELVE YEARS AGO

COLORADO NIGHTS WERE AS BEAUTIFUL and rawboned as the days, only colder. It was early January, and the creek was all but frozen solid. The whole town of Rocky Ford would soon close down until the April spring melt. Everyone would leave except the gold seekers and the Indian traders.

When Rocky Ford Creek froze up, the whole town froze up as well, though most people had already packed up and headed south. Tonight, Jason waited and watched for the man he'd been searching over a year for. He knew the man was here somewhere, and he knew he'd recognize the face instantly. Though the gunfight with the men who killed his family seemed to happen in a blur, the image of the survivor was burned into his mind. The man had red hair and mustache; short, thin build; half of one ear missing; narrow, brown eyes; and a hawklike nose. The face he would never forget belonged to the one man in the world that Jason wanted to kill. Yet he was the one man who could clear his name of murder.

The man named Scoot finally left the saloon, pausing to wrap his sheepskin coat tight, collar high. He shoved his hands deep in his pockets, hat low over his eyes. He didn't seem to notice Jason until he almost walked into him.

"Hey," Jason said quietly.

Scoot stopped and studied Jason as he stood leaning against the wall with one boot heel propped against the wall, knee bent outward. Jason also wore a heavy, sheepskin snow coat and had both hands in his pockets. He kept his face and eyes shaded by the brim of his hat.

"Well? What do you want, stranger?" Scoot said after a moment.

"I've been looking for you for over a year."

"And who might you be?"

"Your name's Scoot, isn't it?"

"Yeah, that's what my friends call me."

"My name's Jason Peares."

Jason stepped out of the shadows and pushed his hat back on his head so Scoot could see his face. At first, Scoot just stood there not knowing who he was talking to. He gazed into fierce-looking, clear, brown eyes that burned into his own. Recognition slowly dawned on him. His eyes widened, and his jaw dropped open. Fear replaced surprise, and Jason pulled his gun from his right coat pocket.

"You're the only man who can clear my name. All you have to do is tell the truth to the sheriff in this town about what happened in Malden. If you do, you'll live. If you don't, I'm gonna shoot you. What'll it be?"

"You think I had something to do with what happened to your family. Well, I didn't. I never killed anybody. That was Max and Daniel. Honest, I never touched them. I was just riding along with the gang. I swear."

Jason stepped close to Scoot, grabbed him by the front of his coat, and shoved the barrel of his gun under his chin.

"I don't care about the others, because they're already dead. You make the difference between me living as a fugitive or a free man. You don't have to tell them you were there when your gang killed my folks. Just tell them you saw your friends pull their guns on me first in Malden, and I shot them in self-defense. You got that, or do I have to end it for you here and now?"

Scoot looked from Jason's eyes to his gun and back to his

eyes, then nodded slowly. Jason followed Scoot up the street to the sheriff's office and stepped in behind him. He felt close to freedom again after a year of hiding during the day and running at night, never knowing who was looking for him, if anyone at all. All he needed was for Scoot to tell the truth about Malden, and he could live free again. Forget the past, forget revenge. He just wanted to live again like a regular person.

Jason stepped aside of Scoot and lowered his gun as they entered the jailhouse. The frontier lawman was an old man with a nearly bald head and a huge, round belly. He sat behind a cluttered desk while his deputy stood against the opposite wall to Jason's left, fixing coffee.

"Evening, boys. What can I do for you? Want some coffee? Oh! You're a Negro, aren't you?"

"Sheriff, this man has something to tell you. Don't you, Scoot?"

Scoot stood there staring behind Jason at the wall, eyes wide, a smile spreading across his face.

"That's him, Sheriff. Right there!"

Jason turned to see what had caught Scoot's attention. What he saw took his breath away. Tacked on the wall to the right of the desk were three rows of Wanted posters. On the third row, fourth from the left, was Jason's own picture, hand-drawn, but very accurate. Under the picture was the story in large letters.

WANTED: ALIVE

by Sheriff Townsend of Malden, Missouri

for the cold-blooded murder of four men.

$50 REWARD

for the return of JASON PEARES to Malden for hanging.

Jason spun back to face Scoot, his mind racing and panicking.

"Tell him the truth, dammit! Tell him!"

Scoot backed against the wall, smiling with vicious greed in his eyes at the prospect of being fifty dollars richer. The lawman moved his huge bulk out of his chair, and his deputy reached for the rifle rack. Jason backed against the door. The sheriff went for his gun, but Jason covered him with his own. All he wanted to do was kill Scoot right now, but he couldn't. Scoot's death would end his last hope of clearing his name. Jason backed through the door, waving his gun from side to side, covering first the sheriff, then his deputy. Jason paused at the door, focusing a hate-filled glare at Scoot.

"You'll pay for this. I swear to God above. I'll make you suffer like my family suffered."

For hours Jason rode without direction, wandering and thinking. He had spent more than a year searching for the only man that could clear his name. Now hope had turned into mist and was gone forever. He felt nothing. There was no more hatred left in him. There was no more anger or frustration. He felt numb.

At least over the last year he'd had a purpose, a reason to keep living and moving, searching for that hope. Now he had nothing. He was an outlaw, a wanted man, with a price of fifty dollars on his head! And it was all because of an unfair sheriff and Jason's own ill-tempered mistake. Now he was running for his life with nowhere to go and no reason to stop running.

Two weeks later, Jason found himself in another Colorado town he hadn't bothered to learn the name of. He flopped himself down on the edge of the boardwalk, shivering against the cold. His belly growled so hard it hurt, but he couldn't even clean up horse manure in the corral for a piece of bread. It was the same situation everywhere he went. Jobs in the dead of winter were nowhere to be found.

He hadn't had anything to eat for three days, but he didn't dare try to steal anything else or he'd likely get shot again. He rubbed dried blood from his arm and wondered how to get the buckshot out. He only hoped the wound wouldn't get infected. He'd been lucky. He lost the chickens, but he didn't lose his life.

He needed a heavier coat or a blanket, but he'd sold all his belongings over the weeks for cans of beans or bread or what-ever. Now all he had was an old, crippled horse he had found along the trail and his father's ancient gun. Heck, the gun had been ancient before the war.

He heard the commotion approaching him but didn't much care. He shivered again and huddled against the edge of the one-story hotel. An old Chinese man scuttled by in the darkness fol-lowed by four rowdy men. He sprawled in the dirt as one of the rowdy guys kicked his leg, but the man just collected his walking stick, muttered apologies, and hurried on into the lamplit street.

The old man wore flimsy clothes and shoes, and he carried only his walking stick and a knapsack. The four bullies crowded around him, pushing and poking him, while laughing and mouthing obscenities. Jason's heart went out to the old man. He certainly knew what it felt like to be bullied and pushed around. He remembered a certain bully in Malden who had stolen his girl. Well, Donna hadn't actually been his girl. Still, the anger simmering in his gut exploded. He'd seen enough of this kind of bullying.

Jason stood up as the Chinese man hit the ground again, and he shouted at the men.

"Hey! Leave that old man alone. He's not hurting anyone."

Jason walked out into the light holding his gun pointed at a man who was about to kick the Chinese man. The old man stood up and waved Jason away, starting to object, but Jason ignored him. The Chinese were always so damned humble anyway. Besides all else, Jason was mad now. Bullies always wanted to pick on weaker folks.

One man pulled his gun and started to point it at Jason, but Jason aimed quickly and drilled him right between the eyes, inches from the old man's head. The other three men pulled their guns and Jason's gun clicked empty.

He stood motionless, unprepared to meet his maker, but suddenly the Chinese man was a flurry of movement. The man's hands and feet flashed through the air, and the first two bullies dropped unconscious within seconds. The third pulled a knife after the Chinese man kicked his gun from his hand. The old man picked up his walking stick, spun it crazy-like in the air, and whacked the knifeman upside the head. Then he ran toward Jason, grabbed him by the arm, and pulled him along after him.

The two went around back of the buildings, then ran into some bushes by the barn and corral. They watched as people came out and found the limp bodies in the street. The three men the old man had beat up were eventually revived and helped, but the body of the fourth man Jason had shot between the eyes was dragged into a nearby barn.

Jason told his new companion to wait while he gathered his old horse, but when he came back, he found the old man doubled over, wheezing in a coughing fit. After a few minutes, Jason helped him onto the horse, and they rode farther into the darkness.

Jason was puzzled by the Chinese man, but the man didn't seem to want to talk. Jason knew if he could learn the kind of tricks the old man knew, nobody would ever bully him again. They camped late, and when Jason awoke, the sun was peeking over the nearby hills and the Chinese man was cooking rice in a metal cup over a small fire. At the sight of food, Jason's stomach knotted up, and he eyed the cup of rice lustily.

The old man smiled and handed the cup to Jason, who dug into it greedily with his fingers. He stopped to breathe when he was about half-finished and noticed the old man watching him. He sheepishly offered the cup to the man, but the elder man just waved it away.

"Hunger is a state of the mind. I eat when I need strength, not when my head tells me my belly is empty."

Jason shrugged and finished off the rice. The Chinese man patted out the fire, then they mounted up and rode off. Dawn of the next morning, they found the body. Whoever the man was, he was dead now, but he had money and a gun and Jason quickly confiscated those.

The Chinese man spoke. "I think you should bury him, then I will say some words for him."

"Bury him? What for?"

"Because I am the elder, and you will respect me by doing what I say. Besides, you are young and strong, and I am old and tired."

"Well, I'm young and tired and hungry. Why don't we just leave him?"

"Hungry again? You just ate yesterday."

"That cup of rice didn't last me very long. I want some real food today."

Jason pulled the gun out from his belt and checked the chamber. It was full.

"I'm going hunting."

"Just a minute." The old man walked over to the horse. "We have food here."

Jason glanced around, searching, then watched the man pet the old horse on the head and behind the ears. His eyes narrowed as the man brought his right hand up close to his head, fingers steeled and slightly bent.

"Ai-shah!"

He brought the bony edge of his hand down hard against the horse's skull with a hollow thump. The horse shuddered, its legs buckled, and it folded down to the ground. Jay took slow, halting steps toward the animal, knowing but not believing it was dead. Then he reversed the gun in his grip and charged at the man.

"You killed my horse!"

Jay swung wildly at the man but hit nothing except the ground. He tried to catch his breath, then rolled over only to see the old man standing next to him, emptying the bullets out of his gun. Jason jumped to his feet and charged, but again he went flying. He spat dirt and grass from his mouth and came in slowly the third time.

The Chinese man held up a hand. "If I can kill a horse with one hand and it weighs ten times as much as you, do you not wonder what I can do to you?"

"Yeah, well, I fight back!"

"First, let me show you something. It may make you not so full of ignorance."

Jason listened to the insult but waited anyway. The man stepped close to him and pointed at his own bare foot. Jason looked down, first at the three or four long hairs that drifted from the top of the old man's freckled, bald head, then at the man's foot.

"Do you see the bug crawling on my foot?"

"No, and I don't care either."

"Then take a closer look."

Jason had the briefest glimpse of the old man's foot flashing up and felt no pain as his head snapped back. He saw only a brief flash of light before darkness engulfed him.

Hours later, Jason felt the heat of a large fire and awoke slowly to see large chunks of horse meat cooking over a bonfire. The old man sat nearby, apparently sleeping in a sitting position with his legs crossed. Jay groaned as he tried to get to his feet, then rubbed the bruise on the left side of his face. His companion opened his eyes at Jason's movements.

"Now you see how boldness and uncontained pride can hurt you. You saw me as a harmless, sick, old man, but I surprised you, eh?" The Chinese man laughed. "I did not need you to save me, but I appreciate the thought."

"Yeah." Jason nodded. "Can you teach me that trick?"

"It is no trick, young man. It is merely the age-old art of discipline of which self-defense is a small part. But yes, I can teach you how to use your feet and hands as weapons, but it will do you little good until you learn to use your mind. You will need to learn mental discipline first."

Jason picked up a piece of horse meat the man had skewered on small branch sticks and cooked. He sat down next to the old man and calmly bit small pieces. He handed the meat to the old man.

"No, young man," he waved aside the meat. "You try to impress me, but I know you are hungry. Your hands shake and I can hear your belly growling. Please, have your fill, then you will be strong enough to bury the carcass and carry our food."

"Carry it? Where to?"

"California."

"California! How're we gonna get there? Remember, we're eating the horse."

"It is only a few hundred miles away. We will walk."

"Walk to California? That'll take years!"

"You have somewhere else you would rather go?"

Jason rolled his eyes, stuffed the rest of the meat in his mouth, and tossed the stick into the fire. He buried the remainder of the animal's carcass in a pit dug with only a small tree branch and his hands, then sat around thinking, fidgeting, and getting bored while the cooked horse meat cooled enough to carry. The Chinese man just sat with his legs crossed and his eyes closed. Jason was studying the vein pattern on his third leaf when the old man finally spoke.

"Will you be still!"

"I'm bored, and I'm tired of sitting here. When are we leaving?"

"Ah, yes. I forgot you are in a hurry to go somewhere."

He jumped up and started wrapping their food in the dead man's shirt and pants. "Well, let us go, then."

"Sounds good to me, but we'll have to salt and cure this meat soon or it'll rot." Jason staggered under the weight of the two packs of horse meat. "I was getting cramps from sitting in one place for so long."

"Young man," the old man began.

"Jason. My name's Jason."

"Very well, Jason. Boredom is a state of the mind, as discipline is a state of the mind. When you learn discipline, you can conquer the mind, and the feeble body causes no discomfort. Discipline, young Jason. You need a lot of discipline, I can tell. You do not belong out here in this hard frontier life. You will not last long without discipline."

"How do you know where I belong?" Jason gasped through

heavy breaths. "I'm just as much a man as anyone else. And at least I don't let people push me around."

"Yes, you are a man with your mouth and your gun, but you do not have control over that which surrounds you. You run into trouble, but you do not conquer it. Discipline will allow you to control through your mind all that is around you."

"So," Jay huffed, gasping for air, "Can you teach me some discipline?"

"It cannot be taught. It must be learned. And your pride is too big, young man." The old man stopped walking. "You know," he said, as if the thought just occurred to him. "Pride is a man's greatest enemy. It will cause you to kill, or it will cause you to be killed. When you have conquered your pride, you will have learned discipline."

They walked for several days. The old man had a few small coughing fits, but Jason became concerned one morning when the man suddenly bent over in a fit that continued several minutes. At first, he just watched. After a moment, he dropped the remaining pack and grabbed the old man by the shoulders. He tried to comfort him as the man trembled through the fit. Five minutes later, the fit subsided, leaving the man weak and gasping for breath.

"Are you sick or something?"

"I have a cough, but not for much longer. That is why I go to California, so I can see the ocean where I came from. My days are short."

"Your days are short?" Jason asked. The old man nodded. "How short?"

"Very short."

"Well," Jason hesitated. "Can you teach me, er, I mean, help me to learn some discipline? You know, before we...uh, before we get to California?"

Jason grabbed the pack of meat and followed the old man as he resumed walking.

"You are already learning."

# CHAPTER 14

J ASON DISCOVERED THE MAN'S NAME was Liu Wang. He worked on the railroad for a greedy man who treated his immigrant workers not much better than slaves. One night, Liu Wang escaped into the night.

They traveled at a leisurely pace that consumed a few miles each day. As they approached a town, Jason desperately searched for a reason to avoid going in. Normally, Jason avoided all towns in the daytime, but they needed coats and blankets and shoes. Besides, he didn't want to have to explain why he was afraid.

Jason and the Chinese man stepped up on the boardwalk to get around the mud patch in the street left from the rains of the previous night. A man and woman stepped out from the store just before they passed, and Jason and his companion walked close to the edge of the boardwalk to let them by. The man stepped in front of the woman and bellowed at them.

"Step off, and let the woman pass!"

The Chinese man stepped off the boardwalk, into the mud, and Jason stepped as far left as he could without falling off.

"I said step off!" the man shouted.

Jason looked around. "But there's plenty of room."

The man shot out his hand and pummeled Jason in the chest. "All the way off!"

Jason waved his arms frantically but splashed down in

the mud on his rump. He jumped up cussing. The man on the boardwalk sneered and flexed his gun hand.

"You wanna talk about it, boy? Go 'head, draw!"

"Jason! This is not necessary. We go, quickly!"

The Chinese man grabbed Jason by the arm and turned him away from the challenge.

"Come back here, boy. You got a gun. Use it! I said draw!"

Jason kept walking, but the man went for his gun anyway. Jason spun at the sound and drew his gun. He saw the old man move at the same time. He flicked something metal at the man just as Jason centered his gun on the man's chest. The man screamed in pain as the star blade sliced into his wrist. Liu Wang pulled Jason by the sleeve.

"If you would have simply stepped off the boardwalk, this would not have happened."

Jason looked back at the man almost too late. The man reached across with his left hand and pulled his gun free. He shouted and aimed. Jason drew quickly—reacting out of panic—and shot him once. The old man turned at the same time and reached for Jason's gun, but he was too late. The woman screamed, knelt by her fallen escort, and started pointing toward Jason and the Chinese man as they ran between two buildings.

Voices followed, but confusion reigned. Jason and Liu Wang disappeared into the thickets and found their pack where they had left it. Again, his companion doubled over in a coughing fit, while Jason watched helplessly. Each fit lasted longer than the one before, and the old man was always weaker each time. He was watching Liu Wang die slowly right in front of him, and there was nothing he could do about it.

"You did not have to kill him," he said after a while. "If you would have just stepped off the boardwalk."

"But there was plenty of room for all of us," Jason protested.

"And so you killed a man for it?"

"He was going to shoot us—shoot you!"

"Jason, Jason." The old man nodded sadly. "You have not learned anything. You do not use your head and walk around trouble. You have to always puff out your chest and walk into its hard wall."

Jason looked at the ground and said nothing. The elder looked at him for a moment, then stood up and walked away. Four days later, they came upon another town, but this time Jason decided to avoid trouble.

"Look, I'll just wait for you here. Okay?" Jason said.

Liu Wang just grabbed him by the arm and pulled him to the back door of the general store. It was locked, so he started to pull Jason around to the front.

"No, wait. You don't understand."

"You are afraid. I understand that. But you have to face this fear. We go."

He pulled Jason again. They were about to round the corner onto the main street when Jason suddenly yanked back on his arm. Again, he started to speak, but his companion yanked back the opposite way and pulled down and to the left. Jason was propelled forward, almost losing his balance, past the boardwalk where four men were examining some papers. They looked up as Jason tripped in front of them.

"Well, I'll be damned! That's him, ain't it? Turn the page back some."

One of the others flipped pages back until he came to one that they all studied.

"Sure does look like him," said another.

"Hey, you! C'mere a second."

Jason glanced at his companion and slowly walked toward the men. His mind raced for something to do, but what? What would Liu Wang do?

"Looky here. We got you!"

One of the men pulled his gun as Jason stepped up onto the boardwalk. Another handed him the Wanted poster with his face drawn on it. He hesitated, then reached for the paper, all of a sudden knowing what to do.

*"Walk around trouble," the old man had said.*

Jason looked at the paper, then smiled and turned and walked over to the old man as he stepped up onto the boardwalk.

"Look at this. This guy looks just like me!"

The old man just shrugged, and they looked back at the four men. Jason gave the paper back to one of the men.

"Is his name George too?"

"Boy, can't you read? This here fella's name is Jason Peares."

"You mean that outlaw? How much is he wanted for?" Jason asked, eyes wide in surprise.

"Fifty dollars," said another.

"Wow!"

The old man grabbed Jason by the arm, but one of the men stopped them.

"Just a minute. He looks so much like him, ain't nobody gonna know the difference if he's been eatin' lead."

Jason hesitated, glancing from one to the next and watching them consider the merits of their partner's idea.

"But he's wanted alive," Jason said, pretending to be scared.

"Dammit, he's right. We would o' shot the wrong man."

"Yeah."

Two men put their guns away, then the third and fourth shrugged and did the same. Jason and Liu Wang turned and walked up the boardwalk to the general store. The old man leaned toward him and whispered.

"Very good, young Jason. You went around the wall this time."

They went into the store and traded the silver coins for some warm clothes and coats for the coming snow. When they walked out, one of the bounty hunters was walking toward them. They stepped off the boardwalk to go around him, but the man stepped off also and stopped in front of them. His three confused companions watched from the next store but made no move to join him.

"You think you're slick, don't you?" the man said. Then he mocked Jason, "Is his name George? How'd you know this fella is wanted alive if you can't read the paper? Either you're a smooth-talkin' conman or you're Jason Peares. Why don't we take you in and find out for sure?"

Jason saw the look in the man's eye and knew he couldn't bluff his way out twice. He couldn't let them take him in either. He spread his arms innocently and shrugged.

"Well," he said. "You figured me out."

The man smiled. "Maybe you're pretty good with that gun."

Jason smiled back. "Yeah, actually I am."

He looked around. His breath grew short, and his heartbeat raced. He gently pushed Liu Wang out of the way and for once the old man didn't argue. He just reached into a small pocket near the front of the cloth belt holding up his pants. Jason saw the metal glint in the sunlight. The man facing him saw it also and went for his gun. At the same time, the other three watchers stepped forward and went for their guns. The man facing Jason grunted as the star blade pierced his upper arm.

Jason drew his gun and started shooting. Wang stopped in mid-swing before releasing his second blade and just stared at Jason with disbelief and surprise on his face at the speed of Jason's quick-draw. Jason met the stare for only a second.

"Let's get outa here!" Jason shouted.

Jason stepped forward and shouldered the wounded fourth man to the ground as he fumbled for his gun. Liu Wang grabbed their supplies and ran with Jason close behind. A gunshot sounded from somewhere and Jason saw blood erupt from the old man's left arm. He stumbled but didn't fall.

Jason whirled around and aimed at the source. The man wore a star on the lapel of his coat, and Jason hesitated. No way he would shoot a lawman. That would just get him into more trouble. He didn't shoot, but the lawman did.

Jason screamed as the bullet tore into his right shoulder. Pain and fire spread as he felt himself falling to the ground. In a cloud of pain, he saw Liu Wang throw a star blade at the lawman. Two more gunshots sounded, then darkness and silence consumed him.

Much later, Jason awoke with a start, and the pain immediately took hold. He screamed with the effort of moving, but Liu Wang just held him down.

"Be still so I can get the bullet out."

"Just go 'head and let me die!"

"You are not going to die."

"Well, it sure feels like it." Jason ended the sentence with a wail as the old man cut deeper for the bullet.

"Be still. Pain is just a state of the mind. Like hunger."

"No! Just leave me alone!" Jason tried to twist away, but the old man held on tight.

"How does this feel?"

Liu Wang grabbed onto the left side of Jason's neck and squeezed hard. Jason's eyes bulged as he tried to squirm away from the new pain. He brought up both hands to pry the man's hand away, but the pain increased. He screamed and twisted and clawed to no avail. Finally, the man let go and Jason lay still, gasping for air. He rubbed his sore neck with both hands while Wang just smiled at him.

"I thought your arm was so painful you could not use it?"

Jason just looked at his wounded right shoulder and stopped stroking his neck. The old man nodded.

"Where is the pain now? In the neck, yes? Your mind tells you that the pain is in your neck, not in the shoulder as before. So control your mind. Tell it the pain is not real. That is what mental discipline is all about."

Jason looked at his traveling companion. The neck pain was subsiding, and the shoulder was coming back as a dull throb. The man leaned back to tend to his shoulder, all the while lecturing about pain.

"Your body hurts, yes, to give you a message. Once you get the message, just tell your mind to ignore the pain. Think about something else. Then there is no pain. No pain! Ignore it as you would ignore an insect, a pest. It is only a message, a hindrance. Your body must work despite the pain. Your life may depend on it. There is no time for crying and whining. Ah, there is the bullet."

His companion held the distorted piece of metal between his finger and thumb for Jason to see, then tossed it into the fire.

"Now prepare yourself. I am going to fire the wound."

Jason flinched as Liu Wang reached for a smoldering ember. Then he screamed as the man touched the ember to the wound. When it was over, Wang helped him to his feet. He tried telling himself there was no pain, but his shoulder still ached. That part of him hadn't gotten Liu Wang's message.

Jason said, "They'll follow us, you know. And they'll have horses."

"So they will just pass us in the night and not know where we are."

They walked. The sun went down, and they changed directions several times. Jason pulled the packs from the old man and threw them over his good shoulder. It was then Jason recalled that his companion had also been shot by the sheriff's first shot. He looked at the old man's leathery arm. He had simply torn off his sleeve and tied it around the wound.

Jason hiked the packs higher on his shoulder. The strain caused a dull pain in the wound in the opposite shoulder, but he said nothing as they walked through the night. The dull pain blurred into nothing, like a pest to be endured and ignored but not caught. Mile merged into empty mile, day into empty week, mountain into empty plain. Another rainy day arrived, like the day before and the day to follow, when Jason gave in to his curiosity.

"How do I know when I have enough discipline?"

"You need a lot of discipline, young Jason. You did not tell me you have trouble with the law. You thought I would try to get the reward?"

The old man chuckled and reached into his pants. He untied a small brown pouch and tossed it to Jason. Inside, Jason found a dozen gold nuggets and several gold coins.

"This must be worth a fortune!"

"Far more than the fifty dollars you could earn me. It was given to me by a dying friend who said to me, 'If you cannot use this, give it to someone who can.' Now, I pass it on to you with the same words."

"Well, you're not dead yet."

"I do not have long. While I live, I will teach you how to live, because you are a good person, not a murderer."

He paused for a few moments.

"To answer your question, you will never have enough discipline. It simply cannot be measured. You have learned a lot already. You walk in pain and bear the weight of our packs without complaint. And you now spend the hours of loneliness in thought, not in restlessness."

Jason considered the man's wisdom. Thanks to his companion's teaching, Jason did, in fact, feel like he had changed quite a bit over the weeks. He couldn't exactly explain how he'd changed, but he felt different inside. He felt more grounded, less panicked at everything that happened to him. He felt more in control.

Liu Wang walked in silence for a while before continuing, then he chuckled.

"The biggest test will come when you face the pain of the heart. When you can conquer that, then you will have enough discipline."

Jason had the distinct feeling Wang left that test open-ended, as if he would never conquer that test, as if no one ever could. He considered the old man's words. He owed his survival to his companion. True, he was still running from the law, but now he was leading the chase instead of the chase pushing him in random directions. He was running, but no longer running scared. Still, there was so much he wanted to learn—how to throw those star blades and do all those fancy foot and hand moves. He said as much.

Liu Wang nodded. "It took me twenty years to learn all that I know of using the feet and hands. The skill is not in the star blade, but in the hand that throws it. A stick or knife can be equally deadly for one who knows how to throw it. Yes, I can teach you, but my time is short."

Jason learned quickly, eager to learn everything as fast as he could. Yet, the old man taught less each day and slept more each night until one morning, Jason woke up alone.

"I knew you wouldn't make it through these mountains," Jason said as he scraped dirt and rocks over Liu Wang's body. He gathered the old man's personal sack and rummaged through it for something to mark the grave with. He had only one extra pair of threadbare pants, a small book written in Chinese, a small bag of rice, and six star blades.

He took the star blades out and kept them, then put the whole sack on the grave as a memory marker. Jason fingered the star blades, examining their razor-sharp edges. Then he stood up, removed his hat, and bowed his head.

"Lord, please take care of the old man because he took care of me." As an afterthought, he added, "He kept me running, but not running scared."

# CHAPTER 15

## TEN YEARS AGO

AS USUAL, JASON WANDERED INTO town after dark. Eyes were less observant during the night, and in this town, everyone seemed too busy to notice one stranger passing through. Tonight, Jason was looking for a room. He was tired of sleeping on the ground and eating out of cans. He was tired of raiding birds' nests or trapping little varmints. He wanted a real meal and a real bed.

He couldn't tell how large the town was in the dark. Only one street other than the main street was lit at night, but as he wandered among all the pedestrian and horse traffic, he got the feeling there were many other streets. Jason rode among the shadows cast by burning streetlamps and stopped at the first of several hotels. He tied his horse to the hitching post and stepped up on the boardwalk. A woman standing outside the hotel stepped forward to greet him. Jason eyed her without expression. She wore a low-cut, nighttime party dress, wide and blooming at the bottom. Her jacket was open and most of her enormous breasts bubbled over the top of the dress. Her curly, shoulder-length hair glistened red in the lamplight.

"Lookin' for a little fun, cowboy?" she asked.

"No, ma'am. I'm just looking for a place to eat and sleep."

The woman turned her nose up and looked Jason up and

down. He wore a simple, brown plaid wool shirt and brown corduroy pants under his unbuttoned, knee-length, black overcoat, and a wide-brimmed, black hat rested low over his eyes, deepening the shadows across his face. He saw her gaze linger on his newly acquired double-gun holster and her expression changed to desire as if skill in bed could be determined by perceived skill of gun handling.

He knew that, like most people, she judged him to be a gunfighter. He certainly had honed the skills of the trade over the past three years on the run. His reputation had grown also. With the dispatch of several bounty hunters, the bounty for his capture had risen to two hundred dollars. He walked past the lady of the night and into the hotel.

"I'd like a room, please," he said, removing his hat at the desk. He placed two coins on the counter in front of him. The clerk looked up from his books and shook his head.

"Sorry, friend. You'll not find a room here. Maybe you will a couple of streets over."

"My money's not good in this hotel?"

"Your money's fine, but not your skin color. Sorry."

Jason looked at the man for a few seconds, then picked up his money and headed out. He felt no need to be angry as the experience was not new to him. He walked up the street leading his horse by the reins and stopped at four more hotels. The clerks told him the same story each time, most times not as politely as the first. The last man he spoke to suggested he try either of the two hotels for non-White miners.

Jason checked the first, but as he walked in the front door, he could hardly call it a hotel. It was simply a single, large room with a desk for reception. There were no rooms or walls or even bunks. There was only floor space completely packed with men in their bedrolls. At the second hotel, there was a long line of men waiting to get in. Black, Mexican, and Indian miners covered from head to foot in soot and mud stared at him through tired eyes as he walked by.

He continued past and went back up the street to a small

diner where he had seen some non-White folks eating. He entered and looked around. There was one empty table at the back of the small room, so he removed his hat and headed for the table. A muscular Black man sitting in a group of four spoke as Jason passed their table.

"White folks eat up the street, boy. Half-White is still White as far as we're concerned."

The man's companions agreed with nods and chuckles.

Jason stopped beside their table. He glanced at each man for a brief second, then concentrated on the speaker.

"I didn't ask for your opinion, mister."

Jason flashed back in time to where it all started in Malden, Missouri. He remembered the bully in that restaurant who had taken Donna from him. Tonight, he wasn't in the mood for bullies. He'd done a lot of growing up in the last three years, and he was neither intimidated nor afraid of the bully who had spoken to him. The man started to stand up, but Jason quickly palmed his right gun. He put his left hand on the man's shoulder and pushed him back down in his chair.

"I got no problems putting a hole in your head, mister. Whatever law exists hereabouts won't even come around here to find your body until daybreak. Now, eat your food and mind your own damn business."

The man held Jason's gaze for a long time before apparently deciding not to press the issue. Jason went to his table and the kitchen girl brought his food. He ate in silence and remembered a different working girl in another part of the country. He wondered how Donna began working for the gentleman who owned the saloon in Malden.

*Did she enjoy her job or was that all she could do? Where is she now? Maybe she moved on or got married and had a family or something.*

He wondered how Donna got the gentleman to take such a risk as to break Jason out of jail. *Maybe he loved her.* He'd seen stranger relationships on the frontier, but he couldn't even begin to guess why Donna had cared even a little about a seventeen-year-old, half-Black, half-White kid from the mountains. He dismissed the thoughts with a shake of his head and finished his meal, then paid and left.

He retrieved his horse and walked back up to the main intersection of town. Though there were no rooms to be had, at least he'd filled his belly with hot food. He had no other choice but to hit the trail again and get far enough up into the hills to find a quiet spot and bed down for the night. He was just about to mount up when he saw a group of men, all wearing gray long coats. He watched them walk out of a building and stride confidently across the main street and into a restaurant.

Realizing he had covered every street in the town except the main street—mostly because that street was lit up by the most streetlamps, Jason could see that the building the men had exited was a hotel. It was far classier than the other mining hotels, yet one of the men in the group was a big Black man. In their gray long coats, the group looked like a posse, and that gave Jason an idea. He tied his horse to the rail and brazenly walked in the front door of the hotel.

"Sure, we got rooms," the young man said as Jason dropped three coins on the counter. "I'll bet you're with the posse."

"Of course," Jason lied. "I'm joining up in the morning."

"Yeah? Well, these guys all come in here throwing money around wanting special treatment."

"I guess money talks."

"Especially Marshal Gallagher's money. You know what they say about him. He never quits, and he always gets his man. You're lucky to be riding with his posse."

"Yeah, I know."

"I hear in almost fifteen years of huntin' outlaws, none of his men have ever got themselves killed. That half-breed gunfighter ain't got a chance."

Jason stared at him, then glanced over the young man's shoulder where he was pointing his thumb at several Wanted posters tacked to the wall. One of the posters bore Jason's likeness on it, except it was the youthful, round face of a seventeen-year-old kid. Life and reality had hardened him. The youthful innocence and wonderment at all the new and exciting things on the frontier were gone. The fear of all the unknown danger was gone as well.

The young man handed him his room key and said, "He kinda looks like you a bit."

Jason scrunched his eyebrows up a bit. "Who? Marshal Gallagher?"

The young man chuckled and waved away Jason's joke. "No, the outlaw."

"Well now, don't go tellin' *that* to anybody. I don't want to get shot by my own men by accident."

"Yeah, that would be a bad start to your day." He chuckled. "You ain't met them yet?"

"Nope. I just got a letter tellin' me to be here and join up in the morning. Meet the marshal and his posse and all that. So I don't even know all the details yet." Jason paused for effect and feigned interest. "I don't suppose he told you why they're after this outlaw. I mean, two hundred dollars is a lot of money, but hardly worth bringing out a whole posse."

"Pa says that outlaw killed the marshal's son a while ago, over in eastern Colorado. He was a lawman too. Sheriff Gallagher was his name. I heard Jason Peares and some Chinese mercenary ganged up on him. The outlaw shot him in the head twice in cold blood."

Jason stopped breathing for a moment but recovered quickly. It had to be the same sheriff who shot him two years ago, the one Liu Wang hit with his star blade. Maybe someone came along and plugged the young man later, then conveniently blamed it on the outlaw, Jason Peares.

"Oh, well, I suppose it's bad luck for him having the marshal on his trail." He shrugged. "Where's my room?" He glanced at the stairs running up the back wall.

"It's upstairs, middle of the hall, along this wall, on the right side." He indicated the wall behind him.

"Thanks. And don't tell them I'm here yet. I want to get to sleep early, and I don't want 'em wakin' me. Okay?"

"Sure, mister. And I gave you the room next to the marshal's. I heard he's got two other Coloreds on his posse too."

Jason nodded his thanks, wondering why the youngster needed to share that information with him. Perhaps he wanted Jason to feel better knowing he wasn't the only Colored man on the posse. Or maybe that was his way of explaining why he was allowed to stay in the expensive hotel. Regardless, Jason retrieved his pack from his horse and went upstairs.

If he bolted and ran now, he would surely draw suspicion. The moon was almost full and tracking him at night would be child's play for the posse. He'd have to play along and hope to sneak out after midnight when everyone was asleep.

Jason dumped his pack on the floor beside the door, then lay on the creaky bed and waited. If the young man downstairs mentioned anything about him to the marshal when he returned, Jason would have to fight a hopeless shootout with an overwhelming number of lawmen. He felt trapped. He was on the second floor of a building with no clear path to escape. There was only a front door and a back door. He checked outside the window and discovered a significant distance between the hotel and the next building and a very long drop to the ground. Escape out the window would only lead to some broken bones.

So he settled in to wait. He took a deep breath to steady his nerves and remembered Liu Wang's lessons on patience. Finally, he calmed himself. Infinite patience was his greatest weapon. Life's challenges were amusing sometimes. Right when he considered himself somewhat safe, he discovered a posse had been hunting him for two years, and he never even knew it. Not just any posse, he now knew, but the most successful posse west of the Mississippi.

*He always gets his man.*

Now here he was, in the same town and in the same hotel, lying in the room next door to the room where the man who hunted him would sleep.

He tried to recall his encounter with the sheriff. As he and Liu Wang tried to escape after Jason shot the bounty hunters who drew on him, the young man ran from behind the building and started shooting. Jason remembered hesitating, not wanting to shoot a lawman. He certainly remembered being shot, and he remembered seeing Liu Wang throw a star blade. He vaguely recalled hearing other shots, so he knew someone else had joined the fray. By that time, Jason was lying flat on his back. Maybe someone else had bushwhacked the sheriff. Jason sat up in his bed as he recalled another vague memory.

He lay back down. It hardly mattered. The Chinese railroad worker was not alive for the marshal to exact revenge on. Even if he was, it was clear that Gallagher blamed Jason for the death of his son, just as surely as if Jason had killed the sheriff with his own weapons. Now he had to live with the fact that the marshal held him directly responsible. The marshal would hunt him down until he caught him or until one of them was dead.

There was just no way he could defeat the entire posse. There were at least eight of them, perhaps more. He knew what he had to do.

*Run.*

Life's challenges were also rewarding. Had he bypassed the hotel and hit the trail again, he would never have known they were pursuing him. One more day and they would have caught up with him. At least now he knew who they were and why they were hunting him. He had a few hours to make a plan and get a six-hour lead on them. Even as he began to make his plan, he heard footsteps pounding up the stairs and angry voices in the hall.

Jason crept to his door and eased it open a bit so he could see through. There were nine men in the posse and all of them wore badges pinned to their coats. They were old too, some probably more than twice his age of twenty. He studied their faces and memorized their features as they passed his view.

The stairwell came up in the center of the hallway. Half the posse had rooms on the opposite side of the hall, but the last three coming up the stairs turned toward Jason's side. All three walked past his door. The first man was tall and stick-thin with a mass of curly, red hair mushrooming from under his hat and blending into his mustache and beard. The second man was a bear of a man, nearly seven feet tall. He had dark brown skin and his hatless head was shaven completely bald except for a sinister-looking Mohawk strip of black hair in the center of his skull.

Jason knew the third man was Marshal Gallagher. He was half a head shorter than Jason and was a stocky man with streaks of silver-gray in his hair and beard. Severe crow's feet framed his serious, deep blue eyes. In passing, Gallagher looked right at Jason, or rather at the narrow gap of his partially open door. Jason involuntarily took a step backward even though he knew Gallagher could not see him.

The lawman's face and eyes burned into his memory. This was the man who hunted him, who wanted to kill him. At first, Jason wondered what kind of man would continue a manhunt for two years. But in that one-sided eye contact with the marshal, Jason instantly understood the fierce commitment of the man. He knew he had momentarily caught a glimpse of a man who had loved his son fiercely—a man who would do anything to avenge the death of his son.

Jason closed the door quietly as the three men went into Gallagher's room. He lay on his uncomfortable bed again and listened to the voices through the clapboard walls. Mostly, he listened to the angry, hate-filled voice of the man who hunted him.

"He's close. I can feel it."

"We'll pick up his trail in the morning," said a high-pitched voice. Jason sensed that voice belonged to the thin, redheaded man.

"Tomorrow will be a good day for a hanging." The voice that spoke was powerful, with a deep, rich timber. Jason figured it must belong to the big Black man.

"There won't be a hanging. He killed my only son, Bo. I'm

going to shoot him dead. I want to look into his eyes when I kill him."

"Can't do that, Marshal," the high voice said. "We're lawmen. We *gotta* give him a trial. Of course, if you want to make him suffer, you can always drag him behind your horse all the way back to town, then try him for murder. Then stretch his neck in the noose, nice and slow."

"There's not going to be any goddamn trial," Gallagher shouted. "I'll hunt that murdering son of a bitch to the sands of both oceans until I find him. There's nowhere he can hide. I don't care if it takes a whole year, or ten, or twenty, or *fifty* years. I'll find him someday. You hear me? And when I find him, I'll shoot him dead! There'll be no words, no questions, no explanations. I don't care if he's old and gray or crippled or a reformed preacher man. He's a *dead man*, Bo! That I promise."

"Marshal," the deep voice counseled. "You get careless and start riding for revenge, you'll get yourself killed and some of us too. You get into a close quarters gunfight with him, and people are going to die. It's inevitable. He's real fast."

"He may be fast, but if I'm close enough he won't outdraw me." The marshal's voice paused. "Did you know that there's a little spot right between the eyes, about an inch above the eyebrows? If you shoot a man there, the bullet blows through the part of the brain that controls every muscle function and the whole body just relaxes. No matter how fast he is, he won't be shooting back."

There was a long pause before Jason heard Gallagher summarize his fate.

"I don't care when or where. There'll be no words, no questions, and no explanations. Anyone who gets in my way is dead too. Do I make myself clear?"

Jason listened to more talk and planning for nearly an hour before the redhead and the Black man went to their own rooms. He waited two more hours before gathering his pack and leaving his room. At first, he planned to move as quietly as possible, but a single creaking floor slat would betray him and alert the posse.

Instead, he closed his door loudly behind him and walked to the stairs. His boot heels pounded on the wood slat floor.

He heard the snoring stop and start again as he headed down the first few steps. To his right, a door opened, and he heard the metallic sound of a gun being cocked. He froze as he heard Marshal Gallagher's commanding voice.

"You there."

Jason tilted his head up slightly, but kept his face hidden under the brim of his hat. His right hand balanced the pack on his shoulder, but his left hand hovered over his gun butt, out of Gallagher's sight. The marshal was silent for a few long seconds while Jason wondered what the man was going to do and how he could escape if hot lead started flying. Finally, Gallagher relaxed his gun hand.

"Be quiet there. We're trying to sleep."

"Sorry," Jason whispered.

When Gallagher's door closed, Jason let his breath out and continued quietly down the stairs. He realized how lucky he had just been. Marshal Gallagher was not asleep after all. Had he tried to sneak out, he'd have been shot.

Jason crept silently to the front door, glancing over to see an elderly man asleep in his chair behind the counter. He guessed it was the father of the young man who had given him his room. Before opening the door, he grabbed the bell so it wouldn't ring, yanked it from its string, and laid it carefully on the floor. Then he went out into the night. He tied his pack quickly and mounted up, heading for the edge of town. There he stopped long enough to break into a general store and load up supplies for what he knew would be a long chase. Next, he rode by a saloon and made off with another horse so he could switch up on the long trail.

He had heard the marshal's plans and knew they would start after him at first light. He had almost a six-hour lead, and now he had supplies and an extra horse. He was as well prepared as they were, and now he could run them around in circles, doubling back on his own trail many times. He smiled to himself in the darkness as he wondered if their commitment to capture him was as strong as his own commitment to live.

# CHAPTER 16

GALLAGHER FUMED AS HE TOSSED the table full of food away from him. Mrs. Rhodes screamed, and her husband came running in from the other room. He started to speak but froze when he saw Gallagher's gun pointed at his chest.

"Why didn't you tell me Jason Peares was in the hotel?"

"What? Here?" The man looked around in bewilderment as his wife ripped off her apron and ran to her husband. "I didn't know. I swear to God above, we didn't know."

"Your kid knew."

Mr. Rhodes glared accusingly at his son who stood by the door to the kitchen. The youngster shivered with fear. "But he said he was one of your posse."

Gallagher holstered his gun and walked over to the younger Rhodes, but the boy cringed away from him. "And how did he know we were here?"

The boy stammered for words as Gallagher's blue eyes bored into his own.

"He just came in looking for a room, sir, and I asked him if he was with you."

"You asked him?"

"He was wearing guns and all, just like you, Marshal. And he had a coat like yours."

Gallagher closed his eyes and shook his head in exasperation. "Our coats are gray, young man. His was black. I saw him in the hallway lamplight." He turned to Bo Madison.

"He was right in the next room, Bo, and he probably heard all our plans." Madison nodded. "Dammit! I had him in my gunsight when he went downstairs last night making all kinds of noise."

Bo Madison nodded again. "I heard him too. Didn't think nothing of it. Had he been sneaking around, I would've suspected something."

"Yeah, he knew that too. He's real smart. That's for sure," Gallagher said, shaking his head. "I didn't see his face. I didn't know it was him."

Bo Madison turned to the younger Rhodes. "You saw his face." The boy nodded. "You didn't recognize him?"

"He don't look like the picture anymore, sir. Well, not really."

Gallagher looked at Bo Madison and raised his eyebrows. He went into the reception room and retrieved the Wanted poster, a bottle of ink, and a quill. Bo Madison uprighted the huge buffet table with a single hand and motioned to the younger Rhodes to come over.

"How is he different?" Madison said.

At the young man's instructions, Madison drew in a thin mustache and a sparsely unshaven look about his chin, then narrowed the face a bit and drew in a hat.

"And his eyes are different too."

"How so?"

"Well, I dunno, Marshal," the boy shrugged. "Kinda like yours except brown."

Bo Madison studied Gallagher's for a moment, then drew the eyes of Jason Peares clearer, narrowed a bit with the slightest hint of crow's feet, not indicating Gallagher's age, but showing the experience of a young man living the hard frontier life of an outlaw on the run. He drew sharper eyebrows and a furrow above the nose, giving the eyes a deep piercing look.

"He's trail hardened, Marshal," Bo Madison said, holding up the poster.

Gallagher nodded. "Not a kid running scared any longer." He studied the picture of the outlaw. "This one's going to be hard to catch. Wire the judge back home and have him put up a bond for a larger reward."

Bo Madison nodded. "How much?"

Gallagher picked up the ink quill and added a third zero to the amount on the Wanted poster. "Two thousand dollars."

Another deputy stepped through the front door of the hotel. "Marshal, he stole supplies from the general store, and we think he stole a horse too."

Gallagher watched Bo Madison walk over to the door and kneel down to pick up the bell that Jason left beside the door. He held it up for all to see. "He's smart."

"And he's well equipped now too." Gallagher sighed, finally accepting the opportunity had slipped through his fingers. "Well, if this work was easy, anybody could do it. Let's get after him."

Jason spotted his pursuers' tracks several times over the months. It had been eight months, and still they pursued him. The posse was relentless. He backtracked several times. He went around mountains, across deserts, through rivers and streams, and even over granite outcroppings that had to be almost impossible to track a trail on. Any other posse would have given up long ago out of sheer frustration, but not Gallagher. The man possessed a dogged persistence, and Jason knew the man would never tire or quit.

Jason was down to one horse. He lost the other horse two weeks earlier when the animal stepped in a snake hole and broke a leg. He knew the lawmen would be able to trade for fresh mounts at nearly any town. Jason figured he might get lucky and trade for a fresh horse if he came across an outlaw hangout, or he might just as easily get shot. Just because he was an outlaw didn't necessarily mean he could expect acceptance or camaraderie with other outlaws. With or without a fresh horse, the posse would wear him down eventually. It was time for a new strategy.

He gazed ahead toward the Sierra Mountains in the distance. California was a long way from Colorado, and he knew he was gambling his life on the hope that at least some of Gallagher's posse had wives and families.

*Will they be willing to chase me over the mountains with the possibility of being cut off on the other side for several more months during the winter snow?*

Jason's horse trudged ahead in the blistering wind with its head almost to the snow on the ground. His situation was desperate. At times, Jason dismounted and tried to lead the horse, but he made even slower progress in drifts that were up to four feet deep. He had long ago lost the trail and now his horse was making its own way.

He rode the animal slightly uphill in an attempt to get up along the ridge line, but the head-on wind whipped the falling snow nearly horizontal against them. Jason knew the freezing wind would be howling along the ridge also, but at least up there the horse would have a less strenuous trail in shallower snow. He glanced down into the valley far below and knew the deceptively smooth snow was many feet deep. He could not hope to ride down there.

He turned the animal back and tried to zigzag his way up the hill. It took three more hours, but finally he topped the ridge. Holding his hat down against the fierce wind, Jason looked back along the many miles he had covered. From high up in the snowswept mountains, he could see the entire panorama below when the snow occasionally let up. Snow blanketed everything. It occurred to him he should still be able to see the posse. They'd likely be only five or six miles behind him. When the curtain of falling snow let up briefly, Gallagher and his posse were nowhere to be seen.

Maybe they turned back or made camp to wait until the snow stopped. He leaned over to pet his horse, but the animal shuddered violently and sank to its hind quarter so suddenly Jason had to step from the saddle to keep from falling over. The horse whinnied loudly and shuddered again, then collapsed and fell over sideways. That's when Jason saw the blood. In a flash of desperation, he knew what had happened. He spun, dove behind the nearest tree, and drew his only gun from his belt. In the distance, he saw another flash and ducked as he felt the bullet slam into the tree.

*How? How? How?*

His mind screamed for answers. Somehow, Gallagher had outsmarted him and had found an easier trail to the ridge. It never occurred to Jason that the marshal might be familiar with the Sierra Mountains. They were so far from Colorado, but the posse could easily have tracked other fugitives into the same mountains over the years.

He glanced again in time to see another flash, but the shooter was over a quarter-mile away on the next ridge over. He saw a flock of red hair blowing in the wind and knew it was the tall, slender fellow who had conversed with Gallagher and the big Black man called Bo.

Even as he looked a third time, he saw some of the posse ride down into the ravine that separated the two ridges. Others rode along the ridgeline, and Jason instinctively knew that some-where up ahead, the two ridgelines met. He couldn't see where from his position, but Gallagher must see it.

The red-haired man must have an extremely long-range sniper rifle to be shooting from that distance. Jason frowned. The man must be one hell of a sharpshooter to be able to com-pensate for the wind and accurately land his shots too. He could sit there for hours and shoot at him while Jason had no way to shoot back. Even with his rifle, he'd be lucky to get a hit at half that distance in this wind.

Not that it mattered, since his rifle was in its scabbard under the horse. He tucked his gun back into his belt and wished he hadn't removed his holster. He had only a single gun with six shots and there were nine deputies. For a brief moment, Jason considered crawling over to his horse to retrieve more weapons, but he quickly realized that was just wishful thinking born of his hopeless situation. The man with the long rifle would kill him easily if he tried. Even with more guns, the posse would soon have him in a cross fire. He had no way to win that fight.

Jason had mere minutes to figure out a miracle. He could not fight them for they outgunned him a hundred to one. He could not run back the way he came because the snow was too deep and besides, he had miles of nowhere to run anyway, and they had horses. He was down to only one option.

He looked up the incline to a pile of boulders he guessed marked the northern ridge line that joined the two adjacent ridges. What was over that ridge was a mystery, and he didn't care. It might be a five-hundred-foot cliff. Maybe there was an impassable field of ice-covered boulders. It didn't matter because certain death waited for him where he stood. He made his decision quickly and wrapped his collar tighter around his neck. Then he ran for the ridge.

The wind slackened slightly as he ran through the trees, and he heard the pounding of hooves. He glanced to his right and saw Gallagher leading the charge. Bullets zipped by him as his hunters had trouble aiming in the frigid wind howling horizontally along the ridgeline. He was running with his gun in his hand, and he had a clear shot, so he took it. He aimed at the marshal's head and snapped off a quick shot. In perfect weather, he could have made that shot in his sleep, but he missed. Instead, he hit the man riding slightly behind and to the left of Gallagher. He saw the man's head snap back just before he tumbled from his saddle.

Then Jason was at the boulders on the edge of the ridge. He kept running straight into the unknown and leaped over the edge. Below him was nothing but air.

# CHAPTER 17

FOR A FEW SECONDS, HE found himself floating in midair and felt that panicked feeling one might get when one knows he's jumped to his death but still has several seconds before the impact hundreds of feet below. It was a long time to consider the horror of the fact that you were going to die momentarily. Jason screamed.

The wind buffeted him until he fell into an evergreen tree that bent under his impact and deposited him roughly in the snow below. The world tumbled around him crazily as he rolled down the steep slope until finally, he came to rest in snow up to his chest. When he looked back, he found that he was over a hundred yards away from the posse up on the ridge high above him.

It was cold. Jason hadn't realized how cold it really was until now. His hat was gone, and the wind numbed his face and ears. The wet snow seemed to seep everywhere inside his coat, down his neck, inside his shirt, up his sleeves, even inside his pants. Chest deep in the stuff, he shivered madly.

Jason heard a muffled report of gunfire and saw the first of several eruptions of snow as bullets hit nearby. He knew Gallagher and his men would soon be able to compensate for the wind. Then the bullets would find their target, and he would die. He had mere seconds to get to safety. He frantically looked around for something to hide behind, but there was nothing close to him.

He struggled to move in the snow and almost succeeded in crawling out of his hole and onto its crunchy surface before it collapsed under him again. Then he realized his salvation. The windblown snow drifts on the east side of the mountain were soft and lightly packed with dry snow, but the wet frozen snow under Jason was dense and hardpacked by the wind. He struggled to unbutton his long coat and laid it out in front of him as several bullets puffed up snow near him. Three bullets tore through the coat just before Jason leaped upon it, and his momentum slid him forward a few feet over the snow. Then he stopped.

He tried again, laying the coat out in front of him on the slope and stumbling back a few steps in the deep snow. He struggled forward and threw his weight on the coat as a bullet tugged at the collar of his shirt. This time he slid down the incline and guided his coat-sled by digging first one boot, then the other, into the packed snow.

Jason reveled in his narrow escape, but he picked up speed frighteningly fast. The wind and snow iced his face and pounded his nose and mouth so hard he could barely breathe. He tried to dig his feet into the hardpacked snow to slow down, but the effort was wasted. He shot down the hill on mercifully smooth snow at speeds far faster than a horse could run. Desperately, he stayed with his coat-sled even as a small bank of snow piled up against a submerged obstacle tossed him airborne. He managed to stay horizontal as he slammed back into the unforgiving packed snow, but he gasped as the impact knocked his breath from his chest.

Jason clutched the coat with a frozen grip of fingers that felt nothing. His whole body was freezing. He still tried to dig his boots into the snow to slow his speed, but he couldn't feel his feet. He considered abandoning his coat and trying to tumble to a stop, for surely he was far enough away from Gallagher. But he knew beyond a doubt that he would die without his coat in the middle of this snow-covered wasteland.

The frigid cold ate into his mind, and he began to lose his grip on consciousness. He had no idea where he was or how long he had been sliding downhill. He only knew he was cold. He was beyond cold. He felt a numbing, freezing, bone-chilling cold. It was a dying cold. Then he bounced against something that ripped the coat from his frozen grip and sent him tumbling through the air and across more snow. He slammed to a stop against something hard.

Just before he awoke, Jason realized he was warm. When he opened his eyes, his heart jumped into his throat. A bear stared him in the face, eyes wide and menacing, fangs and claws bared. Jason screamed, rolled away, and reached for a gun or a knife or even a stick to use as a club. But the bear did not attack.

"It's only a rug." A woman's voice spoke behind him.

Jason took a deep breath and looked at the rug again. "I knew that."

Fully awake now, he glanced around and saw he had been partially rolled up inside the bearskin rug, in front of a massive stone fireplace with a raging fire. He also realized he was stark naked.

"Your clothes are there on the chair."

The woman turned away and busied herself over a cooking stove while Jason put his clothes on. He noticed his bag of gold coins was on the arm of the chair also. It was the only thing he kept in his pockets and was now his only possession. Everything else, Gallagher claimed.

"I must say you made quite an entrance. I haven't seen a man around these parts for almost eight months, and here you go and practically fall right through my front door."

Jason studied the woman as she cooked. Rebecca Simmons was her name, and she was a pretty woman, big-boned and matronly, hefty in size. Her gray hair was tied back and when she smiled, she looked years younger than the fifty or so that he guessed her to be.

Rebecca loved to talk, partly because she said she had no one to talk to for months at a time and partly because she loved to tell a good story. She told him the story of her life. Her husband owned a meatpacking plant down near New Orleans when they got the fever to search for gold nearly twenty years ago. They lived the adventure of frontier life and retired to the high mountain country of northern California. Richard started to build the cabin, but his heart gave out before he finished.

That was seven years ago. Rebecca finished the cabin herself and had been living in what she described as a perfect heaven ever since. No one bothered her and few people even knew she was there. She was delighted not to have a neighbor for miles, but every now and again she visited town just to remind people that she was still alive.

When Jason asked what she did for food, she pointed to an unusual rifle mounted with several others above the mantle of the fireplace. When he examined it closer, he found it to be the perfect hunting rifle, with the longest barrel he'd ever seen and a perfectly weighted and balanced stock.

"It's a modified Spencer," she said, "with a single-shot mechanism and a forty-four-inch octagonal barrel. It has a four-power spyglass mounted where the sights would be. I've hit game nearly a half mile away, but a true marksman ought to be able to hit his target at nearly three-quarters of a mile if the wind is right."

"I sure could've used something like this up yonder."

"Really?"

"Had a posse chase me over the ridge and one of them was taking shots at me from over a quarter-mile away. It would've been nice to be able to shoot back."

"Are you in trouble with the law?"

"I reckon I am. Marshal Gallagher thinks I killed his son. The bad part of it is, they'll be showing up here as soon as they find a way down the mountain."

"Did you?" she said. "Kill his son?"

Jason was silent for a moment. "I'm not sure, but I think I might have."

Rebecca chuckled. "Seems to me most folks know who they done killed."

He nodded. "I was shot myself and everybody was shooting everybody."

"So who is Marshal Gallagher? Is he up from the San Francisco area?"

"Colorado."

Rebecca gasped. "He chased you all the way out here from Colorado?"

"He won't quit."

Rebecca just looked at him for a moment, but she had an expression on her face that told him she'd heard enough to know he wasn't a bad man.

"Well, they won't be here until spring. Nearest pass through the mountains is darn near fifty miles south and even that might be too packed with snow."

"Then that's where he'll go. These guys won't quit."

"Trust me, they'll quit. Unless they slide down into the valley like you did, they won't be coming around here anytime soon. You're welcome to stay. Besides, I could use the company. You know, if you're of a mind to stick around."

She said it innocently enough, but still Jason's eyebrow raised in surprise.

"I hope I don't frighten you away with my boldness, but I haven't known male companionship since my Richard died. But I know I'm not young and pretty anymore."

Jason chuckled. "You look pretty enough to me," he said. "And you did save my life. I'll be glad to keep you company for a while."

Jason stayed with Rebecca for a full month before he began to get anxious about Gallagher again. Even though Rebecca was certain the posse couldn't get through the pass, Jason wasn't eager to wait around and find out. He told her about what Gallagher said in the hotel, and he certainly didn't want her caught in the cross fire when the posse caught up with him. In exchange for a couple of gold coins, Rebecca gave him a horse and supplies. She bid him farewell with the Spencer long rifle as a parting gift.

For two more years, he wandered through the northwest and up into Canada before finally finding his way back down to Texas to take up with cattle drives. He hadn't heard nor seen any trace of the lawman after leaving California, so he figured the man had finally given up and gone home.

*Gallagher didn't get his man.*

# CHAPTER 18

## PRESENT DAY

J OANNE STARED INTENTLY DOWN AT the bandaged man in the bed. He stared back through one good eye. The other was half-closed and unfocused.

Finally, she turned to the elderly doctor. "Can he answer some questions, Doctor?"

The heavyset doctor pushed his thick spectacles back up on the bridge of his nose and scratched an itch in his gray, receding hair.

"I reckon I can give you five minutes. This man needs to rest." He pushed his spectacles up again as they repeatedly tried to slide off the tip of his nose.

"Thank you, Doctor."

She waited until the doctor left the room, then went over to the door, closed it, and locked the latch with a key that sat upon the nearby basin stand. She calmly walked over to the bed while the patient watched her as best he could without moving his heavily bandaged head. She glared at him again before sitting down beside him. From her coat pocket, she pulled a pistol, cocked it, and pointed it at the man's face.

"I'm going to ask you some questions, mister. If I don't like your answers, I'm going to shoot you in the face." She paused. "But you probably won't die. Do you understand me?"

The man looked from her eyes, down to the gun, and back again. He said nothing, but his expression told her he understood.

"What's your name?"

The man's speech was heavily slurred, and he took three attempts to make himself understood.

"Bo Madison."

"Mr. Madison, how deep is your hatred that you would ride in here under the badge of a lawman and shoot down unarmed women and children just to kill my man?"

Madison said nothing, just looked at the ceiling with his good eye. Joanne noticed that his half-closed left eye didn't move.

Finally, he murmured. "Not...hunting...him."

Joanne shoved the gun under his chin and forced his head to move. He winced in pain and gasped as she shouted at him.

"Liar! I saw you and that marshal. As soon as you recognized Jay, you all started shooting."

Madison took the better part of half an hour to tell Joanne of the marshal's son, killed by Jay's guns, of the two-year manhunt, of Jay hearing the marshal's sworn promise to shoot him on sight.

"My God," Joanne said finally. "You're telling me that a little girl and an old man are dead, and my father is fighting for his life because of a threat made almost ten years ago?"

Madison nodded his head once and told her of the posse's hunt for the Strange Scalpers who had killed and scalped the marshal's wife. When he finally finished, repeating himself several times to be understood, Joanne realized the doctor was banging on the door to the room. She ignored the incessant pounding.

"Jay thinks the marshal was after him. He left the same day to hunt down the posse. And he won't quit until they're all dead."

Madison shook his head with effort. "The marshal will outsmart Jason Peares until he will have to end his chase."

Now it was Joanne's turn to disagree. "You don't know Jay.

He can be utterly relentless and merciless when he needs to be. And he believes that he needs to be."

"You don't know the marshal."

Joanne narrowed her eyes. "But you do, don't you, Mr. Madison?"

The man nodded. "I do."

"You know how to find him?"

"Find the Strange Scalpers. Nothing matters more to the marshal than finding them. If Jason Peares gets in the way, he will deal with him first, then he'll resume his hunt for the Scalpers."

Joanne pondered his reasoning for a moment. The pounding on the door was now accompanied by shouting from the doctor.

"Jay has been gone for almost two weeks now, and you're saying the marshal would only turn his posse to hunt Jay if he interfered with their hunt for the Strange Scalpers." Madison nodded. "So Jay must still be hunting the marshal since he would have returned if he had caught or killed him." She did not want to consider the other possibility—that Jay might be dead.

Joanne stood and lowered the pistol as she studied Bo Madison. Though he was covered by thick blankets, she could see the bulges in his chest where the doctor had piled on bandages after removing the two bullets from his upper chest. Miraculously, neither of Jay's shots had hit vital internal organs.

Madison's real injury was to his head. Jay's glancing shot off the man's skull had gouged out a groove of bone almost exactly through the middle of his Mohawk. As a result, the left half of his body was almost entirely paralyzed. He could move his left arm and leg, but just barely. She saw the man twitch every now and again, as if Madison was trying to use his nearly paralyzed limbs.

For a moment, the sight of such a big, strong man reduced almost to helplessness evoked deep feelings of empathy and pity in Joanne. Part of her almost wanted to take care of the man, help nurse him back to health. Then she remembered this was the man whose shotgun had permanently disfigured her father's face. Her father would live forever horribly scarred if he survived his other bullet wounds. Her resolve hardened and the evil glare reappeared in her eyes. She knew Madison could see it also.

He grunted, trying to make himself heard. "I...help...."

"Damn right, you'll help me."

Joanne moved to the door and unlocked it, then stepped aside as the elderly doctor stormed in.

"Now see here, young woman. I—"

"Doctor, get Mr. Madison ready to travel by tomorrow morning. He's going with me to find my man."

"I will do no such thing, miss. And you—"

It was then the doctor noticed the gun that was still in Joanne's hand. The hammer was cocked back, and Joanne made it clear that she was ready to use the weapon. She stepped closer to the doctor and spoke quietly.

"You will do exactly what I say, Doctor. You will do whatever you have to do to patch him up and make sure he stays alive for at least a week. After I find Jay, I don't care if this man lives or dies. Do you understand me?"

The doctor's gaze moved from Joanne's eyes to her gun, and back again. He was clearly seeing a part of this mild-mannered woman that he never would have guessed could exist. He nodded nervously.

"Good." Joanne stepped close to the bed. "Mr. Madison, I'm riding out tomorrow at sunrise to find my man. You'll ride with my posse. And when I find Marshal Gallagher—if he doesn't listen to reason—I'm going to kill him. If you do anything to interfere with me finding my man, I'll kill you too."

Bo Madison nodded once.

Joanne nodded in return. "If you have any influence with the marshal, I suggest you employ it on his behalf when we find him, for everyone's sake. No one harms my man. I don't care what their reasons are."

Joanne made her weapon safe and jammed the gun back into her coat pocket. She spun on one foot, then walked past the shocked doctor without another word as she left the room.

Jay imagined his tired horse stepped finally across the invisible line that years ago someone determined would be the demarcation separating the lands of Colorado and New Mexico. His horse staggered lazily down the road toward the border town and an hour later, Jay dragged his sweaty, sore butt off the animal in front of a kitchen house. He paid for and ate two steak dinners with all the fixings, then led the horse down to the barn for care. The animal probably could not be nursed fully back to health, but Jay figured someone might take the horse in and make its life comfortable, perhaps as a free gift for a child. It still had a year or two of life remaining and could serve as a gentle riding horse.

Jay settled in for the wait. He busied himself around town at odd jobs, mostly at the cattle pens or the barn, but he never strayed from town. He knew that one day next week or next month, Gallagher would ride through here to ask about him, and he made sure everyone he spoke to knew he was waiting for the marshal.

He described Gallagher as a crazed renegade lawman who would shoot first and sort out the innocents later and invited anyone who did not believe him to send a wire to Rosebud for confirmation. He wanted everyone to believe him and trust him so they would warn him if Gallagher snuck into town some way other than the main road. In the end, Gallagher rode right up the middle of the main street six days after Jay's arrival.

The marshal rode slowly with his hat low, shading his eyes against the bright afternoon sun. He had his Winchester at the ready in his right hand, barrel pointed toward the sky. He held the reins loosely in his left hand, but he also held his pistol cocked and ready in that hand. He led his three horses to the barn and walked back up the street toward the saloon. He was alert and aware, pointing his weapons briefly at anyone who walked out of a door or around a corner. The man was taking no chances.

Jay watched the lawman from the window of his second-floor hotel room. When Gallagher walked up the street to the barn, Jay moved out of his room to watch him from the center hall-way window overlooking the street. As Gallagher went into the saloon, he watched again from his room window. Jay checked his guns again and hurried downstairs to the saloon. He wasn't even going to give the man time to drink a whiskey. He had found the man, or the man had found him, whichever, and he was determined to end their ten-year hunt once and for all.

There were no boardwalks along the road, so no one inside the saloon could hear his footsteps in the dirt, announcing his arrival. Jay simply pulled his two guns from tucked in the front of his belt and stepped through the open doorway. He half ex-pected the marshal to be hiding behind the door, so he pointed his left gun across his body to the right to cover the door. His right gun was pointed to his left, chest high, cocked and ready for action.

Jay pivoted to his left even as the marshal sucked in a breath to speak. He focused on the marshal's gun that was pointed at his head while the marshal focused on Jay's gun that was cen-tered on his chest.

"I figured I'd find you here," Gallagher said, staring into Jay's eyes. "Did you know that there's a little spot right between the eyes—?"

"I know. I heard your speech ten years ago when we stayed in the same hotel. I've actually had occasion to use that bit of wisdom recently." Jay smiled when he saw Gallagher's left eye twitch. "Oh, yes. I learned a lot about you in that two-hour period of time. I never got a chance to thank you for letting me know how you planned to catch me. That kept me alive."

"Until now."

Jay stared Gallagher in the eye. "You know me better than that, Marshal. I'll see your intent in your eyes long before you pull your trigger, and you know it. My reflexes are much faster than yours, and you know that too. I'm betting I'll get off one shot, maybe even two or three."

"All I need is one shot. You will surely die, but chances are good I'll live."

"Perhaps you will live, but for how long?"

"I'll take that chance."

"I wouldn't if I were in your boots. My death will be quick and painless. You may live, Marshal, but it's going to hurt a bit, what with my bullets scrambling up the insides of your chest like goose eggs. Who knows, you might get to spend the rest of your days in a bed, on your back, looking up at the ceiling. Now *that* would be a hell of a way to live out the rest of your days, wouldn't it? I'd say that would be downright bad luck."

"I never count luck as my ally. You shouldn't either." Gallagher's mouth twitched in what might be described as half a smile.

Jay smiled in return. "Luck has always been part of my arsenal."

"So what do we do now? Stand here and stare at each other or talk each other deaf?"

"You made your intentions clear ten years ago, Marshal," Jay said. "I'm just waiting for you to blink. Then I'm going to kill you."

He tossed Gallagher a half-smile of his own. He wanted to plant a little seed of doubt in Gallagher's mind. It was the beginning of the psychological battle that might ultimately determine the winner of their confrontation.

The two men stared at each other, neither wavering. Jay saw deeply rooted evil in Gallagher's sky-blue eyes. He matched his stare with his own penetrating gaze that he knew intimidated most men. Around them, the few guests in the saloon had scrambled to get out through the back door. The two men were alone in a now quiet room.

Jay started to speak, but his attention was distracted by a shout in the street amidst what sounded like a stampede of horses. The voice was familiar.

"There he is, Charles. It's that half-breed gunfighter that shot us up."

"Shoot him! Kill him!"

Jay glanced quickly out through the doorway and saw a dreaded sight. Chris Kendrick sat beside Charles Strange on horseback and pointed guns directly at Jay. They had many more men with them than the last time Jay had seen them. Yet even before he looked out the door, Jay had seen the spark of victory in Gallagher's eyes at the same time. The marshal pulled his trigger.

# CHAPTER 19

ROPPING A GUN, JAY SWEPT his right hand up and knocked aside Gallagher's gun as it exploded next to his forehead. The flash was blinding and the sound deafening. Jay blinked his eyes as the first of Strange's bullets whistled by and slammed into the wall on the opposite side of the room.

Jay executed a vicious side kick he'd learned from Liu Wang and caught Gallagher in the chest. Then he dropped to the floor as more bullets shattered the saloon doorway. He snapped off a few hastily aimed shots at the Strange Scalpers, then pivoted on his left foot with his right leg extended, kicking the saloon door closed. Bullets thudded into the door, exploding chips of wood from its surface as Jay leaped over the nearest table. He reached out his hand and dragged the thick, heavy table onto its side to use as a shield.

He heard scuffling near the bar and knew Gallagher was moving. He looked up over the edge of the table and fired twice. Gallagher spun and rolled over the top of the bar, then bounced up again and fired a few ineffective shots into the thick table Jay was hiding behind. At that moment, the marshal was visible from outside through the window next to the end of the bar.

Charles Strange's voice boomed over the gunfire. "He's got the marshal in there with him!"

A hail of gunfire shattered the window over the bar, exploding row after row of whiskey bottles. Gallagher was trapped, and Jay made his move. Knowing he had victory in his grasp, he ran to the end of the bar and reached around, firing his gun until it was empty. Then he casually reloaded his gun from shells in his belt. When he glanced behind the bar, he saw the impossible. Gallagher was anything but dead.

The marshal crouched behind a thick wooden half wall, impervious to all gunfire. The bartender had obviously been well prepared for frequent gunfights in the saloon. Jay sucked in his breath as he noticed the holes in the walls of the barrier.

*Shooting holes!*

Jay whipped his head back behind the bar as Gallagher's bullet exploded splinters from the wood. He yelped as a wood fragment gouged deeply in the skin under his left eye and sent warm blood running down his cheek. Almost at the same time, something crashed through the glass of the window across the room and behind him.

Spinning on his right hip, Jay fired and rolled across the floor, shooting at the two faces that appeared in the window. His first shot hit one man in the throat, but the second man kept shooting despite the two bullets Jay plugged into his shoulder. He kept shooting at the man even as he heard Gallagher's boots behind him and heard the click of the man's gun hammer above him.

Finally, the man in the window screamed as Jay's shot caught him in the face. He pivoted to try and snap off a quick shot at the marshal, but Gallagher's aim was already centered squarely on his chest.

Then the back door slammed inward.

Jay rolled as Gallagher turned his attention to deal with three men charging through the back door. He jumped to his feet and had the marshal in his sights until another of Charles Strange's men loomed up in the window beside the bar. The shotgun in his hands was pointed at Jay. Jay fired until his gun was empty again, then he dove back behind his upturned table for safety.

Quick, but not quick enough, he realized as Gallagher turned toward him after putting down the last of his intruders. He fired twice, and Jay felt a twinge of fire burn across the inside of his right thigh. He made it safely behind the barrier, but he knew that Gallagher knew his gun was empty again.

As he heard Gallagher take two cautious steps across the room toward him, Jay briefly considered trying to reload his gun. But he hesitated. The marshal was probably as expert with guns as he was. He would hear him reloading and would close in for the kill too fast. He considered a knife throw, but that would be next to useless. It would slow the man, but only if his throw was perfect. Even then, it would not stop him. He heard the tentative steps approaching and looked around frantically behind his shelter. Then he saw his other gun, the one he had tossed away deflecting Gallagher's first shot.

He rolled and reached for it as the approaching footsteps stopped. Gallagher had heard his scramble. Jay heard the marshal's boot heel grind the wood floor as the man pivoted and ran back for his cover. He had to hurry.

Jay grabbed the gun and cocked it, then he was up shooting as Gallagher dove behind the bar again, also shooting. Both men fired wild shots and both men missed until their guns clicked empty.

Jay rushed to reload before Gallagher could come after him again. He heard the marshal reloading at the same time, and he slammed his second chamber closed only seconds before he heard the marshal do the same.

"That's three to two, Marshal."

"Yeah? What are we counting?"

"I had you in my sights three times. That's three opportunities to kill you. Only two for you."

"You won't be so lucky next time. How's your leg?"

"Just a scratch. How's your shoulder?"

"Barely nicked me."

"Well, I figure the one with the most opportunities will walk out of here alive."

"Personally, I don't hold much value in the number of opportunities. It's only the number of successes that counts, and it only takes one." Gallagher changed the subject. "But walking out of here is another story altogether. You got a good look at em. How many shooters you figure are out there?"

"Couple dozen maybe."

"And we've got only four guns between us."

"That's right," Jay agreed. "How many shells do you have left?"

"Enough left to put a few holes in your ass."

"No, thanks. Anything back there behind the bar?"

"Lots of shotgun shells, but no shotgun."

Jay looked around the room. "What about the guys at the back door?"

"Three guns and some shells in their belts. Why don't you gather those together, and we'll split up the ammunition?"

"I've got a better idea," Jay said. "Since I can cover both windows and the front door from here, why don't you go get those guns?"

"Hmmm, let me think about that for a second," Gallagher said. "I don't think so," he continued without even a pause. "I'm not going to turn my back on you for even half a second."

"Why not, Marshal? You and your boys would have shot me in the back in Rosebud if I hadn't turned around and saw you. But like the poor marksman that you are, you managed to kill just about everyone else except me."

Gallagher sighed. "That was a mistake."

"Mistake!?" Jay started to his feet, drawing his gun at the same time, but his wounded leg crumbled under him. "You ride into town to kill me and open fire on innocent men, women, and children and you have the gall to call it a mistake? A little girl and an old man are dead, you murdering bastard!"

"You dare call me a murderer, you son of a bitch! You killed my son in cold blood when he was just doing his job, making his rounds. And now you've killed my entire posse."

"Not your entire posse, Marshal. I've still got one more to kill."

"Only if I don't kill you first, outlaw."

"You're a shameful excuse for a lawman, mister. If it would

do any good, I'd have you arrested or hunted like an outlaw. My fiancée was shot. And her father, well, he'll never be the same."

"I told you that was a mistake."

"Save it, Marshal. I'm not interested in hearing more of your lies."

"And how many of my men did you shoot in the back?"

"Back or front, Marshal, I don't care. Your men deserved it and so do you."

"So be it," Gallagher said. "Let's get it done then."

Jay heard him get up and he took aim.

# CHAPTER 20

J UST AS GALLAGHER'S HEAD ROSE above the bar, a fresh barrage of lead came pouring through the window. Gallagher ducked back down before Jay could get a clean shot.

"Four to two," Jay said. Gallagher said nothing.

The sun set quickly, and the siege quieted. Jay pulled his table into the far corner of the room and stretched out on the floor behind it. He checked his leg wound but found the blood had already clotted. It hurt more than he wanted to admit, but if he avoided moving it too suddenly, the wound would not reopen. He'd have to wrap it, but he didn't want to give the marshal the satisfaction of knowing the extent of his injury.

Even as he accepted the wound, other dull pains echoed in a distant part of his consciousness. The bullet wounds to his shoulder and thigh from Rosebud still harassed his nerves, though after almost three weeks he saw no sign of infection. He'd cleaned the wounds the first four days of his pursuit. Also, the right side of his face twitched as he lay still—a reminder of his close scrape against the tree up in Rocky Forest Town—and his butt was sore from almost two weeks of riding bareback.

Staring at the ceiling, he took several breaths and crossed his hands over his chest, a gun grasped in each palm. He calmed himself, and slowly the pain receded into the deepest recesses of his mind, a gnat of inconvenience to be tolerated but ignored. Then he closed his eyes and absorbed the sounds of the night.

The night insects buzzed loudly and Strange's men ate and

drank in safety, without concern for the noise they made. Jay listened to them for a while before they too settled down to respect the quiet of the night. He knew at least half the men outside would be on watch while the others slept. Shifts would rotate later, probably about midnight.

For a moment, Jay considered taking the offensive and sniping at the attackers, but that wouldn't really help their situation any. If he didn't provoke them, he might at least get a restful night with the temporary peace. Maybe then he could think of a new strategy in the morning. Sooner or later, Jay knew Strange would figure out the easiest way to flush them out. Gallagher echoed his thoughts.

"They'll burn us out in the morning."

Jay nodded in the dark. "I figured as much too. They won't do it in the dark with the slim chance that one of us might get away in the confusion."

"I wouldn't bank on them odds."

"Me either. Maybe we can pry our way through the roof."

"He's got a man up there watching. Probably on the roof of the store next door also. The first head to peak through will get plugged." Gallagher paused. "Don't tell me you haven't heard him moving around up there."

Jay didn't answer. He'd missed that detail. On the other hand, he admitted to himself that Gallagher had proven once again why he was the most accomplished manhunter around.

"Well, have you got any ideas, lawman?"

"I'm thinking the back door is likely to have fewer guards."

"Charles Strange is not stupid," Jay countered. "With all the men he rode in with, if what you suggest is really true, I'll bet it's by his designs."

"Even still, if we can rush out the back and maybe hole up in one of the other stores, we'll have a few minutes of respite while they try to get the word around to the front and regroup."

"Naw," Jay said yawning. "He's probably got nine or ten men out back. Although...maybe we could use those dead bodies in here as shields."

"They'd only protect us from the shooters in front of us, not from the ones on the sides. As soon as we turn to run, we'll have to drop the bodies and that's when they'll plug us right in our backsides."

"Well," Jay said. "That only leaves one course of action."

"And that is...?"

"Let's get some sleep. I'm sure something will present itself tomorrow."

"Agreed."

Jay was quiet for a long time. He closed his eyes but wasn't sure if he actually dozed off or stayed awake for the duration. He opened his eyes to the empty darkness, then closed them again. He concentrated on his surroundings and listened for danger, but there was none. All was quiet outside the saloon, as well as inside. He couldn't hear Gallagher's breathing, but he knew the man was still safe behind his protective barrier.

He wondered what Liu Wang's counsel would be. Many times he had advised Jay that there were always alternatives, but what they really needed was a miracle. Finally, he voiced the thought that had been in his head all the previous afternoon.

"I didn't kill your son, Marshal."

Gallagher drew a deep breath but said nothing, so Jay continued.

"I reckon I ought to own up to what was my fault, because I was there, and I was an outlaw. Those bounty hunters drew down on me and I killed them, true enough. But, when the sheriff came around the side of that building, I froze. I was naive back in those days. I couldn't shoot a lawman."

Gallagher snorted his disbelief.

"Your son shot me, Marshal. I was going down when Liu Wang threw his star blade at him. You can blame me if you want because I was there. Maybe I got him killed."

Gallagher moved suddenly, and Jay cocked a gun and waited. A swish ripped the air over his upturned table, and something thudded into the wall over him. He reached up and found the object. It was a six-pointed Chinese star blade. The obsessed lawman had been carrying it around with him for more than ten years.

"I pulled that from my son's jaw," Gallagher said finally. "It was no fancy Chinese blade that killed my son. He died from two bullet wounds in his chest."

Jay sat up suddenly and leaned back against the wall. He reconsidered a distant memory that had been bothering him for days. He started to speak but froze.

He heard a noise, a scrape outside the front door. It might have been cloth against the wall, like someone was creeping along close to the wall, heading for the door. Maybe it was a gun sliding from its leather holster out there. Jay removed his boots quickly and quietly, then ran to the wall beside the door and waited. He heard more sounds outside the door and knew that Gallagher heard them as well. He saw the door begin to open just an inch, then he moved. He grabbed the door and flung it open, then snapped off three quick shots into the three shadows that were framed in the doorway by the dim moonlight. He slammed the door closed again, just ahead of a barrage of gunfire that drowned out the intruding men's wails of pain.

Jay hit the floor and covered his head as splinters of wood sizzled through the air all around him. As soon as the shooting ceased, Jay looked up at the door. It stayed shut, but it was battered by hundreds of rounds of ammunition. Jay knew it wouldn't hold up against much more assault. Several of the horizontal boards were loose, and the top hinge rattled on a single remaining nail. The vertical planks were all loose, some swinging by only partially sunken nails. Jay saw the wall boards rattle and begin to separate. He took a running leap and dove behind his protective table. Finally, the gunfire ceased just after Jay put his boots back on.

"The door's about gone, and the wall won't hold up much longer," Jay said calmly.

Gallagher grunted. "I'd say we're just about at the point of desperation. Any action is better than no action."

Jay was silent for a moment. "That day when your son shot

me, I remembered hearing more gunshots. After I fell or while I was falling, I don't really remember which. I always figured someone else had come around and got the drop on your son. And maybe everyone said I did it because they knew I was there. A week later, when I found more bullets to reload my gun, I realized I was short two."

"So you admit killing my son."

"I reckon. I don't remember much about the shooting except getting shot myself." Jay paused. "All these years, I figured you blamed me for getting him killed. I never knew I actually killed him." He sighed and felt a twinge of regret. "Well, I certainly can't have you following me around for the rest of my days. At least now I know why I have to kill you. And I won't feel guilty about it either."

"Likewise, I'm going to hate not taking the first opportunity to kill you. But while we're trapped in here, I suggest we put our personal differences aside. Our chances of survival are twice as good with both of us alive and well."

He accepted the wisdom of the marshal's words. Although Gallagher was a formidable opponent, Jay had the feeling he would be an even more effective ally.

"Marshal, if I were trapped here with anyone else, I might disagree with you about our odds of survival. But I've heard all about you and your reputation over the years. So I accept your proposal." Jay paused for effect. "Don't mean I'm gonna turn my back on you."

"Wouldn't be smart if you did."

Jay turned his attention to the silence of the room and once again absorbed the quieting sounds of the night outside the saloon. He heard the buzz of the insects, the distant call of a coyote, and the sporadic movement or a periodic cough from the sentries outside. Finally, he drifted into a light sleep, awakening just before dawn as the sky slowly lightened. He lay still until he heard Gallagher stir behind the bar, then he crept over next to the bar.

"Marshal, with the sky lighting up outside and it being dark in here, we'll be able to see them before they can see us. Maybe we can cause some confusion out there and create an opportunity."

"Maybe. We'll sure scare the hell out of the ones still asleep. Besides, as soon as they open up some of those wall boards or if that door comes down, we'll be sitting ducks in here for snipers once it's full daylight."'

"Yeah," Jay agreed. "See if you can take out Strange or his lead man. From the window on the side, I'll hit the guy on the roof next door. If we time it right, we'll have 'em shooting up the front and back and we'll have a few seconds to climb out the side window and maybe get around back and jump those guys."

"Sounds ambitious," Gallagher said.

Jay knew it was a flawed and extremely wishful plan, but Gallagher presented no better ideas at the moment.

Gallagher agreed. "Okay, but we'll only get one shot, maybe two, before they regroup, so make 'em count."

The side window near Jay's upturned table was almost chest high, so Jay slid two chairs under it for something to jump off of when they dove through the window to freedom. The second chair would be useful just in case the first jumper knocked over his chair. Then Jay settled in with just his gun visible above the lower edge of the window.

As an afterthought, he reached behind his upturned table and located the old hat he'd picked up when he first rode into town and squished it on his head as he settled in to wait for the sky to reveal his target. When Gallagher shot his first target, Jay planned to break the window glass so the sniper on the roof next door would be lured to the edge. He would be framed against the light background of the sky, and he would die.

"All these years, you've been living just a week's ride to the west of me, and I didn't even know that little town existed," Gallagher mumbled.

"I've only been in Rosebud a year."

"Kinda makes a mockery of the two years I spent chasing you all over creation."

"Only two?" Jay said, gazing across the room in the darkness.

"I didn't hear about my son's death until a year later, after I returned from collecting a bad man who tried to run down to Mexico. I didn't set out on your trail until I heard about some of your misdeeds a year before we ended up in that hotel together. After you slid down the mountain in California, we decided to turn around and get back to our families. It would've taken us another month or two to find a pass to the other side. With all that snow coming down, I knew it would have been impossible to pick up your trail. I figured we'd hear about you soon enough, then we'd hit the trail again." He paused. "Every time we'd inquire about you, it seems you had already moved on, and nobody knew where. Hell of a life to live on the run like that."

"After California, I spent the next two years riding up in Canada, still trying to lose you. I just knew you were right behind me somewhere."

"Serves you right." Both men were silent for a while. "Thing is, the odds are always against the runner. Sooner or later, he always makes a mistake, and we were always there to make him pay. No one has ever lived the outlaw life successfully—except you." Jay heard respect in the man's voice. "You're the only one who ever got away."

"So what changed your mind after all these years? You have a bad dream about your son and decide to come after me again?"

"Wait," Gallagher said. "Someone's pointing over here. I think they can see me."

He started shooting just before a single rifle fired at his window. He emptied his gun at the men across the street as fast as he could, then he was moving. Just as Jay expected, the sniper on the roof took aim. Then three other men peered over the edge of the roof. There was not just one sniper, but four. Jay fired quickly, but only hit two snipers before the other two ducked back down to safety.

Jay spun and slammed his body into Gallagher's just as the man prepared to leap up on one of the chairs and dive through the window. Bullets from the two remaining snipers thudded into the floor beside them as they tumbled against Jay's upturned table. Marshal Gallagher knew he would have been killed.

Suddenly, gunfire poured into the saloon from all sides. Two planks fell from the front door and bullets thudded into the table beside them. The two men leaped over the table and sprawled in the cramped corner. When they came to rest, their guns were precariously pointed at each other.

# CHAPTER 21

J AY LOOKED GALLAGHER IN THE eye. "After we settle this business with Charles Strange, right?"

Gallagher nodded and moved his gun away. Jay did the same. After a few more minutes, the gunfire died down, and Jay began to reload his guns. Gallagher did the same, but Jay noticed the marshal didn't have enough shells for full chambers.

"How many shots you got left?"

"Nine. You?"

Jay counted the shells in his gun belt. "Ten, plus twelve in the chambers."

"Not much to hold off an entire army."

They both heard the swoosh of a torch being tossed in the front window, brightening the room momentarily and casting shadows as it landed behind the bar. Both men held their breath as they stared across the room, both praying that the flames didn't catch. Their prayers were unanswered, and the fire spread quickly.

Without the need for words, both men started up to go put out the fire, but gunfire forced them back down behind the table. By the time the gunfire ended, the fire had spread over the bar and up the side wall, its hungry fingers reaching up the wall and beginning to crawl across the ceiling.

Gallagher cursed and said, "Now this is not a good development."

Jay nodded his agreement and frantically searched his mind for escape, some option they had not yet considered.

"We'd better think of something, and quick."

"There's nothing to think of," Gallagher said. "We burn in here or we die out there."

Jay cocked his guns and squatted on his haunches. "We may not get the chance to conclude our business, Marshal."

"We may yet."

Marshal Gallagher and Jay locked stares for long seconds, neither man willing to break the eye contact first.

Finally, Gallagher spoke. "Ready to storm the gates of hell?"

Jay nodded. "I'll grab the back doorknob and open. Then I'll provide cover fire while you roll through to the left. Then you cover me, and I'll go to the right."

"That ought to confuse them for all of two seconds."

"Got a better idea?"

"Not right at the moment. Let's do it."

Both men prepared for their dash, then the familiar voice froze them.

"Hey, Marshal Gallagher," Charles Strange hollered. "Why don't you send Jason Peares out? Do that, and I'll let you go. He's the one I want."

Jay looked confused. "You know him?"

"You could say that," Gallagher said. "I know that he doesn't like to lose, and I wouldn't put stock in anything he says. It'll only get someone killed. But let's hear what he has to say. He might give us something to use to our advantage."

"This could be your last chance to get out of here if there's a shred of honesty in the man."

"There isn't."

Jay started to say more, but Strange hollered at them again.

"What do you say, Marshal? I know you don't want to burn in there. Send me the gunfighter."

Gallagher's eyes narrowed as he looked at Jay. "Exactly what is it he wants with you, Jason?"

"I go by 'Jay' now."

"Oh?"

"Yeah. Just Jay."

"If I had a name like yours, I'd change it too."

Jay looked away with a distant gaze in his eyes. Mrs. Travers's last words entered his mind. How many other people are looking for you because of your past? If you don't return, then I'll know you've decided to do the right thing.

"Doesn't matter much. Trouble still comes around no matter what name I use." He focused a contempt-filled glare at Gallagher. "People look hard enough, they usually end up finding me."

Gallagher defused the stare down by changing the subject. "So what's his interest in you?"

"I shot up his gang in Rosebud about ten minutes before you rode in."

"The gunfire I heard." Gallagher nodded. "I was lulled into thinking everything was all right when I saw the townsfolk walking around." He paused. "So you got the drop on them? How? From behind?"

Jay let a half-smile crease the corners of his mouth, but it disappeared before it reached his eyes.

"No, Marshal. I'm not as smart and crafty as you are. I just used my God-given talents. People claim I'm a gunfighter, and maybe I am. I outdrew them." He paused for effect. "All of them."

Gallagher couldn't keep the surprise from his eyes.

"That's right. One of his boys grabbed my girl and put a gun to her temple, so I shot him in the head." He tapped his gun barrel between his own eyes. "Right here, in that little spot you like to speak of. I reckon we could say that you saved my woman's life."

Gallagher looked as if he only half-believed Jay. "You drew down on a man who had a gun to your woman's head?"

Jay nodded, clearly letting the marshal absorb the implication of what he was saying.

"You're good at what you do, Marshal, and I'm good at what

I do. When it comes to gun play, I'm not someone to trifle with. There's not many men alive better at it than I am."

"And Strange never went back to even the score?"

"I don't know that for sure, but I'd guess he wanted to stay clear of Rosebud. I killed two of his men running him out. He wouldn't have known that I left the next day after you or that the sheriff was near dead."

Jay paused for a second as he tried with intense effort to swallow the sharp stab of anger and hatred that suddenly took hold of him. He looked away from Gallagher, but he knew the man would have to be blind not to see it also.

Jay continued. "I figure Strange is a coward. He just terrorizes towns that can't defend themselves and runs away from those where he can't bend the people to his will."

Now Gallagher looked away. "He may be a coward, but he plays his games to win. And if he doesn't win, he'll be a cold-blooded killer. The lowest, dirtiest, most heartless kind of murderer you've ever seen."

"Come on out, Jason Peares! Give yourself up and I'll let your friend live. I know it's getting hot in there!"

"Friend?" Jay snorted. "If he only knew."

Slowly, the possibility dawned on him, and he glanced over at Gallagher, seeing the same conclusion in the man's eyes. Gallagher shook his head.

"Why not? He thinks we're friends. He thinks we actually care what happens to each other. If we can use that to get outside, I can get him in my sights."

"It won't work."

"It's our only chance."

"It...won't...work."

"You don't know that for sure."

Gallagher spun, grabbed Jay by his collar, and yanked him close so their noses were only an inch apart. Suddenly, both men had a gun under each other's chin.

What Jay saw scared him. Gallagher was no longer the controlled, capable lawman with a mission. He was a wild-eyed maniac, breathing short, shallow gasps like he had lost his sanity, and his gun hand trembled violently.

"I know, okay? I know it won't work," the marshal said finally. He let go of Jay's shirt and lowered his gun, the ice-cold look of death back in his blue eyes. He stopped shaking.

Jay started to speak, but a single shot blasted through the broken-down door. Both men ducked farther down behind the table as the bullet chipped away wood from the wall above their heads.

"This is your last chance, boys!" Strange hollered.

A huge chunk of burning debris from the ceiling collapsed into the center of the floor and set it aflame. At the same time, several rows of burning shelves behind the bar fell from the wall and set fire to the bar. Sparks erupted from the falling embers and smoke billowed out the windows. Gallagher grabbed a kerchief from his rear pocket and tied it around his neck, then raised it over his nose. Jay tried to breathe through his shirt sleeve.

"It's now or never, Marshal."

Strange called out to them again. "Maybe I ought to take a little trip back up to your hometown, Jason, and grab that pretty young lady friend of yours. Maybe I'll add her scalp to my collection." Loud guffaws of laughter mixed with the roar of the flames.

"Ain't that right, Marshal? I'll put her scalp on my belt right next to your wife's pretty red hair!"

More laughter was drowned out by another barrage of gunfire. Jay looked over at the lawman, but the man sat staring at the underside of the table, his eyes glazed by tears. When he spoke, Jay could barely hear him.

"If I just live long enough to kill him, I'll die at peace with my demons." He closed his eyes tight, and moisture trekked down his cheeks, quickly disappearing into his beard.

Suddenly, Jay understood the impossible as all the pieces of the confusing puzzle fell together. All the questions he had no longer nagged him, all the coincidences and poor tactical decisions by the marshal. It was all so clear to him now.

"You were tracking them all along." Gallagher didn't respond, so Jay said, "This was never about me, was it? Not about your son?"

Gallagher simply looked at Jay through glazed, watery eyes and shook his head. They sat silently for a few minutes.

"Jesus Christ, Marshal," Jay muttered. "What in the name of God have we done?" He paused. "All those people we've killed."

Marshal Gallagher said nothing.

"How long were you married?"

"A long, long time. Far too long to even think about starting over again." Gallagher's eyes became distant for a moment, and Jay could almost feel the man's pain. "There'll never be another woman like my Lizzy." Gallagher's voice cracked.

"I feel that way about Joanne. 'Cept I haven't quite got around to marrying her yet."

Suddenly, Gallagher's voice was strong again. "Why the hell not?"

"I don't know." Jay shrugged. "Things. Trouble from the past always seems to get in the way."

"That's horse manure, and you know it."

"Maybe, but her pa ran me out of town at gunpoint twice. When I set out on the trail after you, her ma told me not to come back."

"So what are you gonna do, let 'em scare you off? Or are you just gonna run away?"

Jay's anger flared, and he gazed at Gallagher for a moment. He said nothing and the marshal continued.

"I've been in this business long enough to know that men like you, who do what you do...." Gallagher's voice trailed off for a moment. "Men like us, who do what we do, always find it easier to run away from problems, all the while blaming circumstances. It is the nature of our line of work, and only the strongest can stand and face the problems."

Jay absorbed the older man's lecture, partly knowing Gallagher needed to talk himself through his own loss. Another part of Jay admitted he needed to hear it just as much.

Gallagher repeated his question. "So what are you gonna do?"

"I don't know."

"Trouble with you is, you're still young. You still think you're immortal, or that all your life is still in front of you. Truth is," he pointed upward and coughed as the flat bottom of the roiling smoke settled down just above them. "You never know when your time will come."

Gallagher took a deep rasping breath and continued. "Few people in our line of work live to see my age. If you're lucky, half your life is still ahead—maybe less. You'd best quit putting off the important things and marry that woman. Don't let anything or anyone stand in your way."

Jay just looked at Gallagher. "You sound like a misguided man under the false impression that we've got even half a chance of getting out of this alive." He paused as Gallagher glanced at him, then he added, "But only if it rains pretty quick and puts out this fire."

Both men looked at each other for a moment, then broke into wild laughter. After a few seconds, both were gasping for air at the floor, trying to avoid the settling ceiling of smoke.

Jay became serious. "Your wise words are easily spoken, Marshal."

"I'm just saying I've dealt with what you're dealing with. You think Lizzy was happy about me being a lawman?"

"I don't reckon she was," Jay guessed. "So what did you do?"

"Only thing I could do. I told her I was a lawman, and that's all I wanted to be. If she wanted to marry me, she'd have to accept that."

Jay shook his head. "Joanne's a bit less agreeable to that kind of talk."

"Well, I didn't exactly phrase it like I was bossin' her around. I'm not stupid. But I do recall investing in several dozen of those fancy imported roses back then." He chuckled to himself at some distant memory. "Besides, she wore me down finally. Took her damn near thirty-five years, but I finally agreed to quit my job."

"My situation's a bit different."

"Not so different, I suspect," Gallagher said. "You are what you are, Jason. It's not about changing to fit her desires or those of her parents."

Jay said nothing, so Gallagher continued. "The only question I see is, does she want to marry you or not?"

Jay nodded. "When you put it that way, I guess that boils things down to the basics."

Jay was about to say something else when an object flashed in through the window at the bar and thudded across the floor behind the bar. He sucked in a breath and shouted.

"Dynamite!"

# CHAPTER 22

JOANNE'S POSSE OF HEAVILY ARMED men, old and young, arrived at the border town the morning after Charles Strange and his band of Scalpers rode in. Her tracker, an honorably discharged Buffalo Soldier named Gus McGee from the Tenth Cavalry, had picked up Strange's tracks easily outside of Rosebud and followed them due south.

The posse quickly came across the carnage of Gallagher's horses, men, and supplies left by Jay, but the tracks didn't clearly indicate who was hunting whom. In the end, Joanne decided to pursue the Strange Scalpers. She had a wary feeling of trust for Bo Madison's judgment, and that trust gave her some measure of comfort. He figured that wherever the Strange Scalpers were found, Marshal Gallagher eventually wouldn't be far behind. It was clear Jay wouldn't be far behind the marshal.

Bo Madison confounded her. Despite the circumstances, he seemed to be a decent, gentle man, not the murderous savage she figured he'd be. If he really were a killer, she'd be able to justify the hatred she wanted to feel. Instead, she couldn't seem to keep her hatred of the man alive. He was kind and well-mannered and seemed as eager as she to diffuse the conflict between Jay and Gallagher. As she grew to know him, she became more attached to him emotionally, more sympathetic to the unfortunate injuries he would have to live with for the rest of his life, like her father.

During the long trip, Bo Madison had explained in detail the current encounter between the two men and their history. The story left Joanne with a feeling of desperation and hopelessness. In the end, she felt she needed to save not only Jay, but Marshal Gallagher and Bo Madison as well. Hearing Madison talk about Gallagher and knowing Jay like she did, she knew the men could never resolve their differences by themselves. They would hunt each other to the ends of the earth, both blind to their misunderstanding.

The trail of the Strange Scalpers led through several more towns, mostly insignificant little mountain villages and more collections of shacks than anything one might consider a real town. At each stop they learned that the Strange Scalpers left carnage and death in their wake, and at each town, Joanne picked up several more volunteers. By the time her posse rode into town from the northeast, they had grown from fourteen men to twenty-five.

On the hilltop outside of town, Gus McGee produced a spyglass from his saddle pack and let Joanne use it to study the depressing scene in the distance. Her heart felt like it was lodged in her throat as she realized Jay must be trapped in the saloon. It occurred to her that while Jay hunted Marshal Gallagher—who hunted the Strange Scalpers—Charles Strange must also have been hunting Jay.

*What else could be the explanation? How else could they all end up in the same town at the same time?*

Strange and his men were holed up in easily defensible positions across the street from the saloon, in back also, and he had half a dozen men on rooftops of every building near the saloon. Jay's situation seemed hopeless. The saloon was already aflame with thick columns of black smoke billowing out from its two shattered windows and its busted front door.

Even as Joanne turned back to the posse, she realized that several arguments had broken out about what to do. Everyone thought their own idea was the right one. She looked to Gus McGee, but he too was in a heated argument with another man.

Joanne wasn't a soldier. She didn't know how to take command or what strategy to use. The posse was nothing but a gaggle of armed men with no leader and no organization. She had traveled all this way with an army now frozen with indecision, only to watch Jay die because she didn't know what to do.

She turned away from the arguing mob to face the burning saloon under siege. Every now and again, Strange's men fired shots into the saloon, but no answering shots rang out. Strange was going to let Jay burn. She clenched her hands in frustration. She had come so close. Bo Madison had cooperated, had shown her the way, and delivered her to Jay, but then the posse self-destructed to the point of ineffectiveness.

*Or has it?*

She spun around in her saddle, only to find Bo Madison staring at her. He beckoned to her with his good arm. The doctor had makeshifted a harness that hung from the top cover rail of the buggy to keep Madison upright during the long ride. He kept his balance with his right arm and leg, and moved his body when necessary by holding onto a loop of rope hanging from the right side of the rail.

When she reached the buggy, Madison stared at her through his one good eye, his right eye, while his useless left eye pointed off somewhere beside Joanne. She shrugged off her uncomfortable feeling and looked into his good eye.

"You know what to do, don't you?"

Madison nodded. Joanne grabbed a rifle from the scabbard beside the driver's brake and stormed into the center of several arguments. She rammed the stock of the weapon into McGee's belly, and he doubled over with a sudden expulsion of breath. She spun the rifle deftly in her grasp and chambered a round, then pointed the business end of the weapon at the nearest man. Everyone quieted down quickly.

"I didn't come all this way to watch my man burn alive in that saloon out yonder. Now, everyone listen to Mr. Madison. He knows what to do." She paused and waved her rifle among the group of men. She was gambling that none would argue to the point of shooting a woman, but she was also hoping they believed she would shoot them if she was desperate enough. She half-believed it herself.

"Does anyone want to argue with me?" No one spoke. "Good. Now listen up."

By the time she finished, Bo Madison had struggled down from the buggy with the aid of a stout crutch and stumbled his way over to the group. His near useless left leg dragged along with him, and his foot gouged a rut in the soft earth as he moved. His left arm flopped limply at his side as he walked on his good right leg, then balanced most of his weight on his crutch as he hopped forward.

He outlined his plan painfully slow, repeating his slurred speech several times as Joanne tried her best to translate. Then the posse moved off in separate directions, leaving only Joanne and one other young man to guard the horses.

Joanne suffered through the next hour, now wishing she could instantly learn more of that "infinite patience" Jay was always talking about. From the low hill that looked upon the border town, she gazed in the direction of the saloon, hoping her men would hurry into position and do something soon. The saloon had turned into a raging conflagration.

Something did happen, but not from one of her men. She gasped as she saw one of the men across the street from the saloon toss something into the front window. Her heart skipped a beat, but just as suddenly, she saw the object tossed out the side window of the saloon. The stick of dynamite flashed into a tremendous explosion with the sound reaching her a scant second later. The man tossed two more sticks into the window and a few seconds later the entire front of the saloon erupted outward in a gush of flame and wood. Then almost the entire roof of the saloon caved downward.

Joanne heard a rash of gunfire erupt from behind the saloon for a moment, then all was silent. She felt strangely numb. She had come so close, but she knew she was too late. Even if Jay had survived the explosion and the roof cave-in, there was no way he could have survived the final rush by Strange's men from the rear.

*No chance.*

Joanne turned back to the horses as her posse finally engaged Strange's men in front of the saloon. Her patience was short-lived and after a few minutes, she could wait no longer. Since Bo Madison had taken the buggy to town, she jumped onto the nearest horse and tore off toward the saloon.

*I have to know what became of Jay.*

Jay scrambled over the table even as more bullets zipped through the air around him in the thickening smoke. He gagged as he forgot to hold his breath, but he grabbed the stick of dynamite and tossed it through the side window in one fluid motion.

A bullet tore through his right thigh, and he went down on his knee, but Gallagher's strong hands grabbed him by the back of his shirt and hauled him back over the table to safety. Bullets continued to slam into the walls and the table as the dynamite exploded harmlessly outside.

"Are you hit, Jason?"

Jay checked his leg and found it usable. "Just a flesh wound, but it hurts like hell." He took a deep breath as he sat up. "Correct me if I'm wrong, Marshal, but I think things just got worse."

"If they have one stick of dynamite, then they've got another," Gallagher said with finality. "Except next time, they'll wait until the wick burns all the way down before they toss it in here. Ought to be over fairly soon now."

"Then let's get the hell out of here. I'd rather take my chances out back."

"Agreed. Besides, I have one more duty to perform. If I am to die, it might as well be in the act of killing Charles Strange."

The roar of the flames inside the small room was deafening. Both men jumped over their barrier and fled toward the back door. Jay dodged around a falling piece of ceiling board as gunfire from the back of the saloon echoed in to join the front barrage. Marshal Gallagher reached the door first and yanked it open. Jay dove through the doorway and rolled into the sunlight, ending up sitting on his rump back-to-back with Gallagher. The explosion from more dynamite inside the saloon slammed the door shut, and it rattled mightily on shaky hinges. Then he heard a mighty groan as the roof of the saloon collapsed.

Stunned, Jay found all of Strange's men were dead. A figure stepped from behind the next building and Jay had him covered instantly.

"You!" Jay said.

"Clear this side," Gallagher called out behind him. "Nothing but dead bodies. What the hell happened here?"

Jay sat too shocked to answer immediately. Finally, he said, "Marshal, I think you'd better see this."

Gallagher gasped as he spun. "Bo!"

He ran to his friend but quickly realized Madison was too frail to hug. Madison stood leaning against his crutch, holding his rifle with the same hand that held the crutch. Quickly, Jay observed the man and his injuries, his left arm, his left leg, and the expressionless left side of his face. His head was still heavily bandaged, and Jay felt a twinge of guilt as the man looked back at him through only one active eye. He gazed at yet another casualty of his deadly misunderstanding with Gallagher.

Several more men stepped from their positions and walked toward the trio. Jay recognized a couple of the men from Rosebud. He quickly learned that Joanne had led the posse to find him.

The gunfire ceased suddenly from the front. Jay looked around and grabbed up four extra guns. He checked them all and scrounged extra shells for each, then tucked two in the front of his belt and two in back. He headed around to the front of what was left of the saloon. The blaze burned fiercely through the collapsed roof, and the side and front walls were gone, blown out by the second dynamite blast. The intense heat of the fire burned away the early morning chill.

Jay stopped in the street with his front guns drawn and surveyed the survivors of the Strange Scalpers. He wanted to find Joanne, but first he had to finish this business with Charles Strange. He heard footsteps behind him and glanced back to see Gallagher following him, a fiercely determined look in his eyes.

They reached the small band of Strange's men who had surrendered, but neither Charles Strange nor Chris Kendrick was among them. Jay started surveying the surrounding buildings. He didn't have to search long as Strange stepped out from a side street. In his grasp was Joanne, and next to them Chris Kendrick strolled with a rifle carried comfortably in his right hand.

Jay froze. Gallagher stopped short behind him and slightly to his right.

Gallagher whispered, "Shoot him the first chance you get. Otherwise, she's dead."

Jay couldn't answer because Strange would see his mouth move. He knew he just had to wait for the right moment. He wouldn't have the same opportunity as he had in Rosebud, and he could tell Charles Strange planned his approach for that. He and Joanne were too far away for Jay to get a clean shot off.

"Gentlemen," Strange said. "Drop your guns to the ground." They hesitated. "Now!"

Gallagher whispered again. "Take him, Jason. He's going to kill her anyway."

Jay slowly returned his guns to his belt, but he could hear Gallagher sigh out loud as he dropped his own guns to the ground.

"You havin' trouble hearin' me? I said, drop them irons. In the dirt."

"Ain't gonna happen," was all Jay said.

"Look, Jason Peares," Strange said calmly, as if negotiating the purchase of a livestock animal. "You know me to be a reasonable man from our last meeting. Things just got outa hand a bit, that's all. Now, I just grabbed the woman because I don't want you tryin' none of that fancy shootin' on me, that's all."

Jay said nothing. Unlike Hank in Rosebud, who had only been six paces away, Charles Strange stood over thirty paces distant. Jay knew he couldn't chance a quick shot from such a distance. The odds were too high he might miss.

"All I want to do is get outa town. She'll go with me to the end of the road, then I'll let her go. You have my word on it."

"Don't believe him," Gallagher whispered forcefully. "That's how he killed Lizzy, because I let him go."

Jay said nothing, but he carefully considered Gallagher's assessment. What exactly could he do about it? He stared at Strange, knowing the man was lying even before Gallagher spoke. Like the marshal said, Strange was playing his game and he didn't like to lose. Jay had already beat him in Rosebud and if Strange walked or rode out of town here he would be taking two defeats with him. Besides, Jay knew the two men could have already been out of town. He chose to stay, and Joanne was just unlucky enough to be in his way. It was clear to Jay that Strange planned to kill her regardless of the outcome of the stalemate. Strange nodded at Jay's lack of action.

"Well, Chris, I think he's having trouble understanding the rules. Why don't you explain it...to the marshal?"

"Gladly."

The freckle-faced man brought his rifle up and chambered a round. Then he took aim at the unarmed Marshal Gallagher.

# CHAPTER 23

J AY DIDN'T THINK. HE JUST reacted. Without even looking at Chris Kendrick, Jay drew his left belt gun, aimed, and fired, all in the time it took the man to look properly through his rifle sights. Then he calmly tucked his gun back in his belt. The heat from the barrel warmed his gut.

The man gasped in surprise as the shot tore through his throat. He dropped to his knees, grabbing his neck in a vain attempt to stop the flow of blood. Finally realizing he was dying, he tried to raise his rifle again. He got it up halfway before Jay drew the same gun again and shot him high in the chest. Jay tucked his gun away again as Chris Kendrick fell over sideways. He continued to squirm and make gasping sounds.

"That wasn't smart," Strange said through clenched teeth.

"I reckon it wasn't," Jay agreed. "He forgot to grab a hostage. It's like I told your partner back in Rosebud. Uh, that would be the dead one, Charles. She's all that's keeping you alive."

Jay knew he was taking a huge risk talking cocky like he was. He had to set Charles Strange off guard, give him something to worry about. Plant the hint that he was a reckless gunfighter. In reality, he was gambling Joanne's life on the thin thread of hope that Strange wouldn't kill her until he made Jay submit. The man had to get his psychological victory first.

Strange pulled back the hammer on his gun by Joanne's ear. "This is your last chance. Drop your guns. *Now*. In the dirt."

"All right," Jay said quickly. "All right." Jay hesitated for effect as if weighing the consequences, then forced a look of defeat to his face and moved for his guns.

"Slowly," Strange warned. "Fingertips only."

Jay obeyed, slowly pulling the guns from his belt and dropping them into the street. He made exaggerated foot movements to kick the guns away, helplessness apparent in his attitude. When he squared up to look at Strange, he was exactly in line between Strange and Gallagher. That's when Marshal Gallagher made his move. He stepped forward and grabbed one of the guns stuck in the back of Jay's belt.

Strange had a delayed reaction as he finally seemed to figure out what Jay had done. The man's eyes darted to Gallagher's gun, and Jay heard the marshal pull back the hammer. In that fraction of time when Charles Strange's attention was distracted, Jay saw the man briefly considering that Gallagher didn't care about the woman but only wanted revenge for the death of his own wife. He saw the man start to shift his gun from Joanne's head to shoot the marshal.

That's when Joanne made her move. She shoved her right hand up and pushed Strange's gun hand and Jay drew. This was no time for a desperate fast draw. Jay aimed slow and careful. Charles Strange was a big man, but Joanne was slender and wasn't much good as a shield. Without the gun at her head, she was a poor choice of hostage, and Jay saw plenty of the man that Joanne's body didn't cover. Jay's first careful shot hit the big man in his right shoulder and rendered his shooting hand useless. Joanne twisted out of his grip, stomping on his foot at the same time, then Jay emptied his gun into the man.

"No, no, no!" Gallagher screamed behind him. The lawman spun Jay in his grip and shoved his gun under Jay's chin. "Alive! I wanted him alive!"

Jay dropped his own gun and quickly wrestled the marshal's gun away from his face. He saw pure, crazed anger in Gallagher's eyes.

"I know that, Marshal," he said as he nodded in the killer's direction. "I think you'll find him in exactly that condition."

Gallagher looked over at the man sprawled in the street. His eyes flared as he saw Charles Strange move.

Gallagher released Jay and moved slowly toward the wounded man like a mountain lion stalking its prey. Jay followed him at a respectable distance. He reached out for Joanne and hugged her tightly as Gallagher simply stared down at Charles Strange. Jay had shot him carefully, twice in the right arm and shoulder, then twice in the left arm and shoulder, then once in each leg. Strange whimpered and struggled, but he wasn't going anywhere.

"Marshal," Jay called. When Gallagher looked at him, the crazed look was gone, replaced by an empty, ice-cold glare of death. "You might try this."

Jay reached under his right pant leg and pulled out his buffalo bone hunting knife. The blade of the one-piece weapon had a light bluish-gray tint, was ten inches long, and razor-sharp. It was a gift years ago from a grateful Arapaho warrior whose mate Jay saved from slave traders in Arizona.

Gallagher holstered his gun and took the knife. He looked at Jay for a moment longer and something akin to a mutual understanding passed wordlessly between the two men. Gallagher nodded his gratitude and took the weapon.

"Make it hurt," Jay said. "Make it hurt real bad and for a long time."

He turned away with Joanne and walked over where Gus McGee and the rest of Joanne's makeshift posse gathered in front of the burning saloon, fighting off the morning cold. Now that the gun work was finished, a number of the posse and some local townsfolk began carrying buckets of water to the shops next door to the saloon. It was clearly a lost cause, but they had to do something. They couldn't just watch their town burn.

Jay made no move to help them. He just didn't care. He figured all six stores in the row would probably burn within the hour, but it wasn't his concern. All he could think about was all the death he had witnessed and caused, the accidental and intentional killings. He'd been involved in some furious gun work over the years, but never with such a high body count and never with so many innocent casualties, mostly by his own hand.

He looked around the street and saw more death. All of the members of the Strange Scalpers who had not been killed in the gunfight had been hung by the neck from rope strung from the porch cover of the hotel two doors up the street from the saloon.

Joanne seemed to sense his thoughts. "This wasn't your fault, Jay."

"At least the Scalpers won't be hurting anyone ever again."

He glanced back at Marshal Gallagher, then looked around for Bo Madison. He sighed. There were still two more innocents that had to die. No way he could let them ride out of town now that they knew where he lived.

# CHAPTER 24

J AY HUGGED JOANNE AGAIN, AND they walked farther up
the street toward the kitchen house. They ate in silence.
Together, yet alone, with the privacy of their own thoughts.
They were interrupted when Gus said the posse was disband-
ing and he and the others were headed home. Gallagher and Bo
Madison waddled into the eating room about an hour later. They
ambled slowly over to Jay's table, Madison leaning heavily on
Gallagher for support. Jay stood, not knowing exactly what to
expect.

"Is he dead?"

Gallagher looked at Jay and laid the clean hunting knife on
the table.

"Hell no," Gallagher said with a sad but determined look in
his eyes. "At least not yet anyway. He will be by noon, I reckon."

Joanne gasped. "But that's nearly four hours from now!"

"For what he's done, I don't reckon it's long enough. I left
strict instructions. If anyone gives him any assistance of any
kind, even a sip of water, I'm gonna shoot 'em."

Gallagher said nothing more, just stood looking at Jay. Jay
returned the gaze, glancing a couple of times between him and
Bo Madison. Bo was in no shape for a fight, and Gallagher looked
like he'd had all the fight taken out of him.

"And us?" Jay finally asked.

Gallagher hesitated for long moments. "I didn't ride the trail
to hunt you, Jason."

"I realize that now. Still, the fact is a lot of people have died."

"On both sides." The marshal paused. "It was an unfortunate misunderstanding, and I regret that. If I could take back my actions, I would."

Jay closed his eyes for a second, seeing in his memory all the dead bodies. He relived the sight of the little girl bleeding to death, screaming in Joanne's arms, and of the old man who owned the general store, his dead body cradled in the arms of his wife of almost fifty years. He saw Joanne's father, lying almost dead on the ground. Then he remembered shooting Moses Jackson from a great distance. No, he didn't just shoot the man. He murdered a man who was riding to make peace.

When he opened his eyes, he could see by the pained look in Gallagher's eyes that he was also reviewing his dead friends and perhaps the innocent civilians of Rosebud who had been killed by the accidental gunfight. His entire posse was gone. Jay also knew the marshal was thinking about his son, killed years ago at the hands of the outlaw Jason Peares. His pain was clear to Jay, as was his simmering hatred. Such hatred could never be simply brushed aside with mere words.

"I regret these last three weeks too," Jay said. "I wish I could bring those people back to life, mine and yours. But...." Jay paused and focused the penetrating gaze of his clear brown eyes on Gallagher's sky-blue eyes so that his next words would not be misunderstood by any stretch of the imagination.

"But they're dead, and I don't want them to have died for nothing. We have unfinished business, you and me. I'll never feel comfortable letting you two ride out of town today knowing that someday, a bad dream might send you back on my trail. Especially now that I know you live so close."

"I tell you what, Jason Peares. You stay out of my town, and I'll stay out of yours."

Jay shook his head. "That's not good enough, Marshal. I'm truly sorry about your wife, but with regards to your son, I've had to kill a lot of kinfolk who came hunting me. You're far more dangerous than any of them because you're much more committed. I'm not going to let you ride out of here."

Gallagher was too dangerous. He'd be back, Jay knew, whenever the pain of losing his wife simmered away and the hatred over the death of his son took hold again.

"I'm going to tell you this for the last time, mister," Gallagher said. His voice was low and even. "I didn't come hunting you. If you need to kill me, then you'll have to shoot me in the back." He turned away, signaling the end of the conversation, and half-carried Bo Madison to the kitchen house door.

"Marshal," Jay called as Gallagher reached for the door. His hand hovered over a gun butt. "Just so we're clear. The next time I see you...."

Gallagher was silent for a long time before he turned. "I reckon we'll talk first...before we start shooting."

Jay nodded. "The next time we meet, then, I'll let you make the first move."

A glimmer of a smile twinkled in Gallagher's blue eyes. "There aren't many men alive who would think that to be a good idea."

"Perhaps," Jay said. "But if you're the honorable man I think you are, it just might keep the two of us alive."

"Agreed." Gallagher turned and helped Bo Madison out the door.

Jay turned to Joanne and hugged her.

"Let's go home and get married."

Her beautiful, dark eyes flashed with excitement.

He kissed her and said, "And I pity the person who tries to come between me and my wife."

# THE END

If you enjoyed this adventure, check out the next book in the Jason Peares saga at JeffreyPostonBooks.com or wherever you buy books. Please let other readers know what you thought of the book by leaving a brief review at your favorite retailer. It only takes a moment and reviews are very valuable to authors.

# ABOUT THE AUTHOR

Jeffrey Poston is the acclaimed author of the Jason Peares historical western series, as well as the fast-paced adventure thriller series *American Terrorist* and *Call Sign: Raven*. Blending traditional and revisionist historical research, his historical westerns have been praised as "fast-moving" (Kelton) and "exciting, page-turning" (Zollinger) and "among the best writers of westerns" (Biblio.com). His thriller books are lauded as "so realistic," "powerfully intense," and "action-packed page turners." He is a self-described *Rambling Man* and writes his novels wherever he happens to be in his travels.

Find Jeffrey at http://www.jeffreypostonbooks.com/
Amazon.com: http://amazon.com/author/jeffreyposton
Facebook: http://www.facebook.com/JeffreyPostonBooks
Twitter: http://www.twitter.com/BooksByJPoston
Goodreads: http://www.goodreads.com/JeffreyPoston

# ACKNOWLEDGMENTS

As writers, we often go into our creative caves to compose a book, but when we come out, there are often dozens of people who help refine a story and turn it into a really good book. No writer can succeed without this special group of people—critical readers, cover artists, professional editors, marketing and PR specialists, and publishers.

I especially want to thank my critical reader and sounding board, Dr. Stephanie McIver. She's helped me through many of my books, offering insight and analysis that added depth and breadth to my characters and my plot.

Special thanks to Debra L. Hartmann, The Pro Book Editor, and her team for copyediting and proofreading. I also want to give a shout-out to the cover art designers of my books: Deanna Dionne.

I'm also thankful for the active imaginations (and the suspension of disbelief) of all the readers who enjoyed my Western and Thriller adventures. I'm especially grateful to the dozens of beta-readers who previewed the book and sent back invaluable advice. Your help means the world to this author!

www.ingramcontent.com/pod-product-compliance
Lightning Source LLC
Chambersburg PA
CBHW020519120726
47904CB00003B/896